FLIEGELMAN'S
DESIRE

6-13-90

For Meraidee —
with pleasure at seeing
you again.

Best,

[signature]

FLIEGELMAN'S
DESIRE

LEWIS BUZBEE

AVAILABLE
PRESS

BALLANTINE BOOKS · NEW YORK

An Available Press Book
Published by Ballantine Books

Library of Congress Catalog Card Number: 89-91504
ISBN: 0-345-36738-3

Text design by Holly Johnson
Cover design by William Geller
Photo of woman: George Kerrigan
Photo of books: The Stock Market/© 1989 Tardos Lamesi

Manufactured in the United States of America

First Edition: June 1990
10 9 8 7 6 5 4 3 2 1

For Greta

ACKNOWLEDGMENTS

All of us depend on those who've come before us and those who work alongside of us. In my little story I have directly and obliquely referred to some of my companions, but such is my debt to a few that they require naming here. My gratitude to my colleagues Robert Haycock, David Hodnett, and Mary Reid. And most especially I must acknowledge the words and music of Jane Siberry whose world, though far from my own, has inextricably mixed with mine. Thanks to you all.

All Things want to fly. Only *we* are weighed down by
  desire,
caught in ourselves and enthralled with our heaviness.

Rainer Maria Rilke
The Sonnets to Orpheus

FLIEGELMAN'S DESIRE

FLIEGELMAN'S
DESIRE

□

Fliegelman walked the granite canyons that held his city. The day stuffed its hands in its pockets and pulled up a collar against the rain and wind. Things were like that.

He had wandered downtown from his apartment outside the shopping district, and as the numbers of the avenues decreased, he discovered that the shops grew more urgent and opulent. Below Fifth Avenue the shops sported gilt decor on their facades, worn like military medals on aging generals; the weight of the gilt was so heavy that the buildings snapped to under the burden, standing sharp and straight. Through the brightly lit store windows Fliegelman noticed that the shoppers stole glances at the day outside. Looking up from their purchases, they were waiting for a better moment.

It was in one of these lower shops, a large emporium on Second, that Fliegelman saw his desire. He stopped in front of the window, beside himself, and looked hard to make sure he was seeing what he saw. Sometimes Fliegelman saw his desire in unexpected places, only to discover that he was mistaken—he'd spotted somebody else's desire or was duped by a trick of mirrors—but this was indeed his desire, standing in this shop trying on clothes. It had been who knows how long since he'd seen his desire. He had heard from mutual friends about his desire—his desire had a new job, looked great, seemed happy if you knew what they meant—but what they told him was suspiciously vague, and he thought maybe his friends were just being kind to him.

The evening came in late and almost knocked the day down getting set up. The evening felt a chill and turned on all its lights to kindle heat, but the fluorescence and incandescence only warmed the eye.

Fliegelman looked around, feeling vulnerable, the watcher watched, afraid his desire might catch him watching his desire. He posted himself near a column up close to the shop window and pretended to look at the items in the window, the mannequins and their perfect furnishings. He had never had the opportunity to watch his desire from such a distance and through such a frame.

The store, so close to the city's heart, was packed with shoppers, and that crush was a perfect screen for his watching. Had the shop been mostly empty, as on Wednesday mornings when only the rich and listless could afford, the few in the shop then, even those walking by outside, would have seen him standing there, and they would have known he was only pretending to stand there and window-shop. This would have made them nervous and they would have called for security. But now, at the height of the rush near the end of the week, there was just too much of everybody for anybody to notice Fliegelman standing there pretending. Fliegelman himself almost didn't realize he was there, face to face with his reflection. It was an hour of great busyness; not even his desire, always so alert and able to pick him out a mile away, would see him.

He felt safer as the net of movement closed around him. Only the evening seemed to notice him, peeking over his shoulder, but the evening didn't care much about Fliegelman's indiscretions. After all, evening saw this sort of stuff all the time, part of the job, the lay of the land.

So Fliegelman watched in safety as his desire raced between the dressing room and the three-sided mirror, trying on new looks. He wondered, watching the frantic changes of his desire's guises, if his desire was shopping to buy or shopping to look. His desire would rush out of the dressing room, fully newly got-up, turn and pose and turn and pose, and watch every angle and try on different moods with every outfit. His desire was clearly looking for something, but whether his desire was looking for one or two new outfits, or whether his desire was looking for the entire range of possibility, Fliegelman could not tell. He knew his desire well enough to know, he thought, that all this shopping might be the whim of a boredom.

Here was Fliegelman's desire dressed in sporty bright colors, turquoise pants and orange top, pink socks and red sneakers. Turning before the mirror, whirling the loose cotton, his desire was young and gay, an art student perhaps, going to a concert or lecture, intent as ever to be the center in the crowd. Fliegelman had seen this studied carelessness before in his desire. It was an outfit for putting the hands on the hips and throwing back the head and laughing. Walking down the street in this costume, a wind would surely arise to toss his desire's hair so that it captured the sun's blade edges. His desire tried several large shoulder bags with this outfit, matching and clashing bags to hold whatever might be needed, bags that could be tossed into a corner without a thought when Fliegelman's desire decided to dance.

And here was his desire suddenly more serious in severe tweeds with silk beneath. This was dress with working intentions. His desire could work hard, he knew, and appointed so, seemed ready to be tied to a desk all day, go to court, make a killing, buckle down, bid higher, take lunch, keep in mind the bottom line, cut petty cash, conglomerate or divest all interest, make statements and advances, foreclose, rise above the din, stay late and work weekends. Fliegelman's desire meant business. And yet the touch of silk, the off-white collar beneath the practical suit, hinted that business had more at stake. A single pair of tortoiseshell glasses was the only mask his desire needed to complement this avaricious, workaday uniform. His desire sucked the end of a pen, mocking the stand-up conference of reports scrutinized with associates in a hallway. Like so, Fliegelman's desire could go away on business and deduct all personal expenses.

His desire went back into the dressing room to change again. It seemed as if all the clothes had already been selected, waiting limp in the curtained closet. Fliegelman wished he had been there when his desire was picking out the outfits, poring over the racks. What was the expression on his desire's face then, excited and frantic, self-forgetful and bland? Who was his desire dressing for, for what occasion? Surely Fliegelman could have picked a clue from the manner of his desire's choosing. He pushed aside all jealous thoughts; chances are his desire was shopping only for desire's sake. Fliegelman could see his desire's calves and ankles in the gap between the curtain and the plush carpet: sturdy, a little thick, but all the same, graceful and beautiful.

When his desire reemerged in evening wear, Fliegelman took a stun between the eyes. This was a desire he knew well. The garb's material was shiny, reflective, so much so that to be thus attired during daylight's hours would have blinded onlookers with kind, white needles. His desire was dressed for night's illuminations, gathering dull, orange lights and red and green neons and blue pinpoints on the loose surfaces and in the tight clinched folds, a shimmering surface of fabric like the black ocean's waves on a moonless night seen from the balcony of a resort hotel. His desire was languid; his desire did not so much stand as rest upright, balanced, it seemed, by a careful cock of the hips; movement seemed, if not quite dangerous, frightfully unimportant. A glass of champagne held lightly in the same hand with a cigarette might lock his desire into permanence. This was the look of his desire's seduction, and it had frozen Fliegelman before, from across a room at a party, say, Fliegelman content to be frozen at that moment, wishing it might last forever.

Now his desire returned in plain clothes, yet quite orchestrated. In jeans already faded, a softened flannel shirt many sizes too large, thick, low-cut cotton socks and no shoes, his desire was ready to sink into a couch on a cold, bright day in a warmed house, sink with a book or a bit of the paper, sink for hours, shifting only to meet the shaft of sunlight that moved as the day tired. This was Sunday apparel, kick around the house, catch up on chores and stretch like a cat stuff, a hideaway from the world and

enjoy the being alone of it outfit, a uniform of recupera-
tion. In this change his desire might unplug the phone for
hours and refuse the untimely door bell. Fliegelman could
hear the list of things to do that would run through his
desire's head on a day like this—vacuum, clean the stove,
write lost letters, make a list of things that had to be done
the next week—but that list would only be a soundtrack to
the day, a shadow of the enjoyment of doing nothing. It
would be the kind of day that would fall through the
cracks of the other days.

His desire continued to change; there seemed to be no
end to it. Each outfit that his desire tried on brought out
aspects of his desire that were at once familiar and surprisingly new to Fliegelman. His desire dressed for sport in
only the finest, most advanced gear, but somehow his desire
seemed ready not to play, but rather seemed ready to stand
next to the court and show off the well-trimmed legs and
arms and flat stomach after having exercised in secret to get
this condition. His desire wore blacks and grays, a mod-
ernly romantic coat and a long-tailed shirt, jingling thirty
silver bracelets, ready to descend the stairs of an all-night
club and ignore the music, looking almost dead in white
makeup. In lightweight cottons and a big straw hat his
desire would visit the small town where his desire was born,
sit on the porch after dinner with the folks, waiting for the
car of an old flame who'd never left the sweltering town,
stay out with the old flame for hours, raising dust on the
county roads and telling stories of life in the big city.
Change after change his desire was someone Fliegelman
had known for years, yet each incarnation struck Fliegelman
as an imposter of his desire, someone he might call to on

the street only to discover, when the called turned to look at him, that he had been mistaken again.

These were the infinite forms of Fliegelman's desire, and he could not decide which of these forms was the one he yearned for most. For every one of the different desires, there was some part of Fliegelman that fit interlocking to that particular form. His desire had a way with him.

The evening grew impatient with Fliegelman and his standing around. It rattled the windows and walls and domed, close sky of the city—loud, booming. Fliegelman turned around, noted the change in evening's mood.

When he turned back to the shop window, his desire was gone. He waited watching a few minutes, but he knew his desire had slipped out some back way, perhaps having caught a glimpse of him. He headed down the street with the evening at his back like a patient but careful cop on the beat. He was tired suddenly, and he had difficulty keeping the rain separate from itself, the so many drops and the wall of flood that surrounded him.

The unexpected appearance of his desire left Fliegelman out of sorts, and he did that thing we all do: he fell into thinking about things he'd have been better off not thinking. He remembered too much. He thought too much about how the future ought to be. He conversed constantly with someone who was not there. He considered his desire and nothing else, and when he tried to break away from his desire, telling the broken air of his rooms that he had become obsessed with his desire and must puncture that obsession, he became obsessed with his obsession. Somewhere in his life his desire had become embodied, had ceased to be a woman with a name and a family and a history, and had become instead simply "his desire." He could not even call his desire "she" or "her." He rooted around in the story of his desire, but could find no trace of the woman who had led him there, and finding nothing of that past, found only that his desire's embodiment became permanent.

It was at this point that he began to make a fool of himself. Although he kept dodging it, he could think of little else but going to his desire's apartment, not to see his desire, but to stand there. The idea to do this came to him the way a distant relative comes to stay for a long time. He got no explanation and he was unable to ignore it, even though he tried to pretend it wasn't there. But the idea had tagged him and it followed him everywhere, and because he tried so hard to evade the idea of going to stand outside his desire's apartment, the idea was only more dogged in its attention. Fliegelman tried to blame his desire for making him consider such a foolish act, but he knew he had no right to do so; whatever Fliegelman did, he did because he wanted, whether he thought about it or not. Blaming his desire was only his way of making sure he didn't stop short. When one morning he left his apartment, he was saying firmly, though not aloud, that it would be nice to go out into the city, and he'd just see where he found himself.

The day was taking it pretty easy, didn't seem to have a lot to do, propped itself in a corner and surveyed the scene. Sometimes the day was caught up and could afford to loaf. It wasn't that there wasn't anything at all for the day to do, just that all the necessities had been covered and nothing begged to be done. The trouble was that most people would take their cues from the day and do nothing themselves. The day could be very irresponsible.

Fliegelman took the No. 38 streetcar to the garden district. The car was mostly empty when he first got on. An elderly couple sat near the front of the car. Both wore green, woolen hats and leaned on wooden walking sticks, silent and connected. A young woman rocked her child in its stroller, watched from the car's last row by a man who looked as if he might have been riding the car all through the night's last shift. The driver was encased in glass. The only voice on board was that of the taped message announcing each of the stops in an even, disinterested tone. Fliegelman felt at ease and almost forgot what he was doing. But as the car worked its way along the line, two or three passengers got on at each stop and Fliegelman felt more alone. That was the way of streetcars, the more people that got on, the lonelier they became.

He stayed seated on the No. 38 when it stopped in front of his desire's building. He looked down at his hands, which he held palms up in his lap, and feigned reading. Should his desire be standing at the window of 816 and recognize him when the streetcar passed (a highly improbable coincidence, Fliegelman knew), it was important that his desire think his appearance casual.

When Fliegelman got off the streetcar at the next stop, two blocks down, he went across the street to the Café K, where he stood at the counter. Squinting and reading every line on the menu, he ordered the usual. When his coffee came, he chose a corner table near the window, where he always sat. He didn't pick up a newspaper, however. There, Fliegelman thought, at least I didn't pick up a paper. He had always read the paper when he came here before. The bored day drummed its fingers on the window.

From where he sat Fliegelman could see his desire's building. The side facing him had had its windows boarded up in preparation for a new building on the abandoned site next to it, but the new building had never started. The boards over the windows had not been painted, and his desire's apartment looked out with three sets of patched, blind eyes. Fliegelman's desire lived on the top floor.

In the café were two types of people, those with someone and those who wished they were with someone. Fliegelman had an unerring eye for this kind of observation. Three couples and four people alone sat at scattered tables in the café with him. All of them were reading newspapers, quietly and with great intention, as if they had to start each day with the simplest of words to relearn the language of others. The couples sat as close to one another as the width of the newspapers and the shapes and angles of the chairs and tables would allow. They touched one another tentatively, a hand on the other's knee or elbow, looking as if they might be about to point out some interesting item of news. Occasionally they would look up, incredulous. Those alone sat formally at their tables, bolt upright in their straight-back chairs. They arranged and rearranged their coffees and ashtrays and cigarettes. They might have been waiting to be called by the receptionist in a doctor's office.

Fliegelman had known this was how the café would appear, and even seemed to have known what the faces of the other customers would look like. Cleverly, he had left himself out of the picture.

He stared into his coffee endlessly. It had been a mistake to come here. He should have stayed at home in his apartment, should have made other plans. He should not have allowed his desire to make him forgetful of himself, nor allowed his desire to make decisions about his life over which he seemed to have no control. Here he was at the café, sharply reminded of his desire and faced with great embarrassment, and he knew that he'd have been better off not being here, stirring the greasy milk into his coffee.

The couples left the Café K, while those who were alone stayed longer, as they had nothing better to do. Soon they would have to leave, for even a café has only so much patience.

Fliegelman watched the No. 38 streetcar stop directly in front of his desire's apartment. The passengers got down from the car on the side that faced the apartment, the side hidden from Fliegelman's vantage. More and more people were on the streetcar now, and each time the car pulled away it left behind a number of passengers. Some of those let down by the streetcar shot off without hesitation to wherever it might be (these were people capable of ignoring the day, no matter its mood), while others stood by the siding, stunned, considering, wary, as if they had been mysteriously set down there from another planet or another time. Little by little these stragglers gathered themselves, attached a focus to some point and, dazed, followed it.

Fliegelman was looking for his desire to get down off the streetcar, although he was assuring himself this was not so; he had come to this café for coffee, sat at this table and achieved this view. It was a rather nice view, with the sky behind so clear and blushed blue. If his desire got down off the streetcar, it most probably meant that his desire had not spent the night at this apartment, for what would his desire have been doing so early under the day's gaze except returning from another bedroom in another part of the city? Fliegelman both wanted and did not want this to be the case. He excluded the possibility that his desire was still in the apartment he watched now and was with the someone who owned the apartment in the other part of town his desire would be returning from were his desire to get down from the streetcar while he watched. And yet in excluding this possibility, he had to graze it just so lightly. He watched, but his desire did not appear.

He then let his mind fall on another possibility: that his desire was alone in his desire's apartment, still in bed (though not sleeping) or at desire's table with breakfast and the paper. There was something about this possibility that bothered him. The more he resisted imagining the scene, the clearer it became to him, and he realized that it was the solitary nature of the scene that made him uneasy. His desire should not have to be alone, no matter Fliegelman's position. He knew his desire was often alone, sometimes even demanded to be alone, but Fliegelman suspected that his desire was hiding a fear of being alone. His desire ought to be attached.

He got up and left the café. The day in its torpor had not yet decided to promote warmth or briskness, and hovered somewhere in the middle. This confused Fliegelman. How was he to approach the day, walking out into it? It seemed unfair to lean into the day, the day so lax, and yet this laxness was irritating to Fliegelman and made him want to walk at a severe angle. Fliegelman did not notice the others on the street who were busy not noticing him. He stopped at the entrance to a garden courtyard two doors down from directly in front of his desire's building. He was where he kept assuring himself he would not be. He hoped he was inconspicuous. The building, he thought, must have drawn him here through some stupid gravity. What could he do? He watched. He hoped the building, standing there so aloof, might reveal to him why it had drawn him up thus.

It was not the wooden face of the building that held the answers, but what hid behind the facade, the airy rooms and corridors, and Fliegelman forbid himself the thought of entering the building unasked. If his desire wanted him inside, his desire would have to invite him.

But he remembered well enough. His desire's apartment was one large room that served as both bedroom and living room, this connected by a hall to the bathroom and kitchen. The main room was open and provided more space than the apartment could have. The bed, covered in old quilts, was trapped against the far wall, shutting a closet Fliegelman had never seen inside. A couch rested along the longest wall, and a desk sat facing the windows Fliegelman could see from the street below. On the fourth wall stood a narrow table. The table displayed objects that, when Fliegelman thought on them, seemed to bear no connections, yet were so aligned on the table as if to make them inseparable. The table held up a yellow and green coffee cup from a distant land, a paper dinosaur, a wooden doll of an earlier century, a lace antimacassar, a rose vase, four plastic frogs from a five-and-ten, and seven pearls in a glass bowl. Fliegelman had often spent time trying to read these objects. Were they trophies or wishes? Were they a map? They were always out and dusted. On the table in between these objects was space, but the space was as crucial as the things themselves, like the holes of a net and the space that took up most of the main room where his desire lived. His desire had a way with such spaces, a way of making the intangible vital.

His desire's kitchen was cramped, a dining table set snug in an alcove and kitchen appliances circled around the sink under two windows that stared onto the wall of the apartment behind. The walls of the kitchen were hung with pots and pans and juicers and ladles; the glass-eyed cabinets above the stove and below the countertops revealed neatly stacked rows of plates, bowls, glasses, and canisters. The crowded nature of the kitchen made close comfort. This kitchen was a home to tasty cooking, but Fliegelman knew that when his desire was alone, his desire did not cook. His desire only steamed or broiled for others; his desire ate meagerly when not feeding others.

Next to the kitchen was his desire's bathroom, white and black tiled. On the back of the door were his desire's towels and bathrobe. This was the room of his desire's secret scents. When his desire had finished bathing and drying and combing, Fliegelman would go into the bathroom to smell the smells, inhaling his desire's expirations, as if to gather the essence of his desire inside him. The bathroom ran hot and cold.

There was only left the narrow hall that strung these rooms, leading from the doorway to the divisions of his desire's life. Standing in the hall, Fliegelman could feel, like the draft of a canyon, the currents that connected his desire, waiting for his desire, in the center of his desire's life. Here the lists scrambled and dissolved, the catalogue of what his desire wore and where his desire lived and the way his desire spent time gathered into one single room.

Whether he came here, was drawn here, or simply ended up here, Fliegelman was here, and he was beginning to know why this was. He had come here because he knew which of his desires, seen through the shop window, was the desire he wanted. It was the desire of jeans, shirt, socks and no shoes, the comfortable desire. The other desires, work or play or seduction, though he was unable to resist them, could make him frantic, divide him endlessly from the Fliegelman he wanted to be. The comfortable desire was only one of his desire's uniforms, and Fliegelman knew his desire would never discard the others, but this was the desire that Fliegelman had come for. It was a desire he could get to know, a desire that would take him in.

Fliegelman's attention had drifted, and when he reeled it in, he looked up and saw his desire at the window, dressed as he'd hoped, looking down at him. He stared at the ground. There was a small coin wedged between the paving stones near his feet. The coin was hardly worth the effort, but he stooped to it and scraped it out of the crack with his keys. He wiped the coin clean on the knee of his trousers. When he looked up again his desire was gone, the curtains pulled. He wanted to say something to his desire, to communicate all that he was thinking, to reveal why he had come to his desire's apartment, to ease the apprehension in his desire's eyes he had seen in that brief moment. But the right form of saying this did not exist; screaming, phoning, writing, touching, talking calmly over coffee at the Café K, all of these were inadequate. There should be some other form of communication, unimaginable but essential, some way of shattering the space. Fliegelman could only stand there with himself.

The day yawned and laid its head on crossed arms. The day was not sleeping, it was fatigued. Fliegelman looked around. The evening was nowhere to be seen.

Fliegelman was surprised to hear his desire's voice. He had, of course, been thinking of his desire when the phone rang, and as a result was not prepared to hear that voice, as if it were impossible that his desire occupy his thoughts and anywhere else at the same time. He was so busy trying to reconcile the two desires, the one in his head and the one out there in the world, that he'd forgotten to be embarrassed for standing outside of his desire's apartment and being seen by his desire. But no mention was made. His desire had phoned to say hello and to see if maybe Fliegelman wanted to get together to talk. They made plans to see each other near the end of the week; as it turned out, both Fliegelman and his desire were busy for the next couple of days. They arranged to meet at Fliegelman's. All Fliegelman could manage to say, as the conversation wore down and silences crept into the phone lines, was that it had been a long time.

"Yes," his desire said. "It's been a long time."

On the day his desire was to come, Fliegelman sat waiting at his window for over an hour. His desire was always late. He had wanted to see his desire coming down the street, but the door's buzzer cried without warning. His desire had slipped past him. He pushed the button that opened the security door and let his desire in. It was a long three flights of stairs, but suddenly his desire was at the landing and Fliegelman was face to face with his desire. The day went tense all over, held one arm behind its back with the other, shuffled its feet.

It was great to see each other, they both said, it had been too long. Oh, yes, much too long. How silly that it had been so long. It was great to see each other.

Fliegelman told his desire to sit down while he made coffee for them. In the kitchen he could hear his desire moving softly about the living room, picking up things and looking at them. His desire looked great, better than he remembered, had lost some weight.

"How are you?" he asked, craning his neck into the hall. "You look great."

"I'm happy," his desire said. "I have a new job. I feel really great, if you know what I mean."

"I know what you mean," he said. "Things at work are going well. I feel good. I think I've lost a little weight."

"You look good," his desire said.

Things were mostly quiet then, until the teakettle whistled. Fliegelman thought his desire must be standing by the front windows and looking out on the street. He brought the coffee in and put it on the coffee table. His desire was sitting on the couch.

"You look great, you really do," Fliegelman said. "It's been a long time."

"Thank you," his desire said. "It has been."

They both stared into their coffee cups; they talked into their cups. They were being nice to each other, but soon Fliegelman realized that he was pacing the large living room. That's the way it was sometimes for Fliegelman, finding himself mid-pace. His desire also seemed upset, sitting there on the couch, ankles crossed, staring into the coffee. The day cracked the air with a snap of its fingers, tried to rouse itself.

They fought. They fought over their parting, and blame was everywhere in the room, but it jumped about so hectically that it was impossible to pin down. Blame just wasn't going to take sides. They tossed bits of reconciliation about the room, bait to attract more blame, but blame is a short-lived creature that feeds on nothing, and soon the room was empty again save Fliegelman and his desire and the little bits of reconciliation going sour.

Fliegelman knew what was next.

"Why do you follow me?" his desire asked. "What do you want from me?"

He forgot denial.

"Well," he said. "You're the one I'm supposed to want, aren't you? What I mean is this, how would you feel if I didn't follow you? This is my job and your job. Without each other, we'd have nothing."

"We have nothing now," his desire said.

"Sort of," he said. "But that nothing, that's something, isn't it? It's what stands between us. Keeps us together."

"Yes, but it tires me so," his desire said. "This being wanted always. Can't you just want me and keep it to yourself, leave me out of it?"

"I don't see how," said Fliegelman. "That would be pointless, don't you think? I've got to have someone to want, I can't just do this abstractly. We know we can't live together, we've tried that. There are too many things that pull us apart. This is how we live together, by being apart. Why does it bother you so?"

Fliegelman's desire looked out the window, sipped, seemed ready to be gone.

"You don't know what it's like," his desire said. "Even when you're not seeing me, I know you're thinking of me, wanting me. I don't get any rest. It keeps me up."

The day shook itself for a moment, tried to clear its head, couldn't figure something.

"What do you want?" Fliegelman asked his desire. "What can I do?"

"I know what I want," his desire said. "But I don't think you can help me. I think that if I had a bigger house, with lots of rooms, that I might not feel so bad about things, about your wanting me so. You know I have a thousand friends, and I like to have them over, but there never seems to be a place for them, my place is so small. I think it would have to be a really big house. Can you do that for me?"

Fliegelman looked around his small apartment. He knew he could never give his desire a house that was big enough. He lived too meagerly. This had always been a problem between the two of them. What he wanted and what his desire wanted never seemed to get along. His desire craved lavishness. Fliegelman had seen that in the shop window.

"You know I can't help you with that," he told his desire. "All that I have are these few rooms here. That's all I'll ever have. I'd like to help you, I really would, I'd like to make you happy, but I don't think I can."

The day was at the end of its rope. The night, standing just around the corner, pulled its hat down over one eye, and being considerate, came on to relieve the day.

"Listen," his desire said. "Thanks for the coffee, but I have to go now."

"Wait," he said. "I don't think we're finished yet. We haven't figured anything out. We still have so much to talk about."

"I know," his desire said. "But I have to catch my streetcar. It'll be here in a few minutes. We can talk later. Thanks again for the coffee."

Then his desire was gone. Fliegelman heard the front door close. He ran down the stairs and out the door to the corner streetcar stop. His desire got on the streetcar and the doors hissed shut. The last thing Fliegelman saw was one of those stupid tricks. As his desire walked toward the back of the streetcar, the streetcar pulled away from Fliegelman, and his desire stood perfectly still, relatively speaking, neither coming nor going. He went back to his apartment and made some coffee for the night's long shift. Later he thought he heard someone scream outside, but it was only the sound of the streetcar braking.

CONSPIRACY OF THE DAYS

□

The seasons changed places. The rains withdrew, as did their big, scuttling clouds and the sharp days they punctuated. The wet, cold days and their alternating warm counterparts leveled into themselves, even, chill. The city slept under a blanket of fog, close, breaking sky at seven peaks and the tallest building. Uniformity took hold; the days lost their sense of themselves, wandering the streets like stunned buddhists in slack, gray robes. In this way the new season obliged Fliegelman, and he tucked himself safe within it.

He had phoned his desire, but the ring hollowed. He had taken the No. 38 streetcar, but it did not stop at his desire's block any longer, and when he retraced the way to his desire's apartment, he found it blocked by another building's massive newness. He had attempted these follies hopelessly, empty, and gave them up soon. His desire had left him, for good he felt, and he knew it was so in the unshakable way he knew such things, without a doubt. This was a safe season that demanded and gave nothing but the next day much like the one before it.

He spent his days at work, calculating. His office,

though quite small, was in one of the biggest buildings, where some dumb luck provided that he should get the rare window. During the previous season, rainy and full of his desire, the window was an exhilaration that held him and made his work endurable. The grievous lights and shades of the days that passed by his window all rapt him; his work was a smooth rendition of efficiency when the storms of light and showers of rain and cloud besieged his safe, warm office. And added to that, the inexplicable bonus of watching his companions who worked across the broad canyons in opposing office buildings. Fliegelman's office was on the third side of a triangle of offices that bounded a park at their foundations, and from this vantage he was able to watch two walls of office windows. Here he often saw much coming and going during the traffic of dark and light. It seemed that, especially in the rain, with all lights and curtains open, yet feeling enclosed by the bluster of the day, his fellow office workers gave themselves over to observation, heedless that anyone might be watching them as they wilted bored into their chairs, hunched over hushed phone calls, stood opposite one another at sexual attention, gathered in groups and assumed new stances. The weather and the watching carried him through these hours.

Now that the season was soft as pillows, however, work was a haze. The papers he shuffled and checked lost their auras of goldenrod, valentine, and ivory, the carbonating copies now pale wedding pastels. The numbers he had always figured on still worked, falling into their places and adding up to something, but where once the numbers jumped to their formations with cheerful speed and agility, they now hobbled across the pages like retreating wounded. The only brightness was that of the telephone's ring, and he could turn that down to a dull, toothache rumble when needed. Outside his office window the days wafted ghostlike, transparent, mocking. The gleaming stone walls across the way were peeling wallpaper now; the windows drew curtains. Business was slow.

Nights, Fliegelman dwelled in his apartment. Here his life, suddenly populous, lay stacked liked mover's cartons, the memories in musty cardboard collecting age and forgetfulness. It was easier to stay seated than to try and move around the packed rooms. His window chair, looking out onto the big church several blocks away on a hill, was of no help. The days hid the church in a drifting wall of orange light, split sometimes by the blue spark of the streetcar change. He listened and watched, curled into himself.

These were his days and nights; they suited him well, tailored, tapered, nipped and tucked. He liked the city like this, all hidden from itself, as if he lived inside a mountainous cave.

Within the new season's fog there were, on occasion, bright razor days, two at a time usually. These bright days Fliegelman disliked, for they never agreed with him, but it wasn't until many weeks into the slow, soft season that he saw a pattern emerge and a conspiracy of the days he could not touch.

This is how it started. It was a Friday, a slung low to the ground time of the afternoon, around three. The day eased and stretched, hung around the water cooler, then pulled its hat from its face, and lightness was everywhere. Ignoring the calls of his desk and watching the sky for ghosts, he was not amused. The light had trouble with the glass and granite towers of the downtown canyons, but managed to invade, breaking sharp on mirrored windows and rusted walls, illuminating keen pieces of sidewalk and flashing yellow on the green leaves of plaza trees. Trapped, and happy to be so, in the office's cool comfort, Fliegelman watched the warmth descend on the city's interior.

He saw the great exodus. The light seemed to suck his office mates from their heavy corridors out onto the silvering streets, as though a dire warning had sounded. They left behind mountains of business, as they jostled manically downward and outward. The sudden filling of the streets ended suddenly, when the packed streetcars and street's cars left for homes outside the canyons. Their hurry was painted by eagerness. Normally, during the week, business land would be dark when they all left, some officers staying close to midnight, but it was further than usual from evening by an easy hour, and light swallowed the hollow places.

Fliegelman, so used to his dark life since his desire's departure, shirked the light and stayed as the last one, walking the plush, blue-dimmed halls of the offices, peeking into the cubicles of the extra executives and musing aloud on their general desires, trying to guess their lives from their belongings. Trash cans offered clues, as did snapshots and paper clippings, but Fliegelman was stumped by the clues he found, and soon began to feel that there was a larger picture that he was trying to construct, one that involved the people who worked with him. It had to do, nagging goaded him, with why they left so early on this Friday, and wasn't it an awfully familiar scene.

He wandered, courting his suspicion. The building, bereft of so many, was now at home with itself. Machines, unattended, buzzed, whirred, clicked, calling to one another, and the empty offices were more perfect with these sounds. Doorways were wind tunnels. Plants' leaves shivered in the wake of the winds that were always hidden when the offices were bodily invaded.

In this secret planet, the offices big now, Fliegelman returned to his own office and laid his quandaries on the desk to inspect them. No matter how he hooked his suspect ideas together, they all implicated the calendar, so he paged through that, returning over and over again to Friday. Friday, Friday, Friday. He saw the buildings eject all the workers, pushing them out the doors and into the street as tired shopkeepers do when closing. He saw it again. Then again. He flipped the calendar to the previous Fridays and felt the breath of the conspiracy on his neck. Each Friday, the day had lightened up, and everyone had gone home early. Each Friday for as long as the season had been changed. He skipped around the other days of the week, Monday, Wednesday, Tuesday, Monday previous, Thursday, but those days stayed mute and consistent and gray. It was always Friday. He was sure that was it, but as he sat there proud of his find, that pleasure gave way to more uncertainty. He walked to the window and looked over the empty canyon, which would stay deserted days until Monday when business, as usual, would return. That was it. He sat down. He paged and paged. Saturday and Sunday, Saturday and Sun— He thought back to weekends. Here was his conspiracy. His city had conspired, through some under-the-counter contract, to bring full, warm light to the weekends. The aged fog lucked the weekday job. It was like hiring the youthful to work the arduously retail hours of Friday's night, all of hectic Saturday, and Sunday's busy anticlimax. Surely, he thought, the chamber of commerce was behind it all, cheerful cynics.

He saw it in one frame, the view from afar of a broad landscape, multitudes of everyone rushing about, climbing and pushing and kicking. There was no foreground in this picture, no intimate tragedy or suffering in the corner, only a detailed and hivelike background. Keep them gray and at work all week, pent up in their cubes, and then release them to the weekend and with them sun and brightness. Fliegelman hated it, for having recovered his weekends in search of his conspiracy, he remembered how he despised them. He pulled his curtains against the advancement.

He stayed at the office because his heart was black and heavy in light of the afternoon's expectations, and he felt easier in the office's temperate cushion. Watching from the high windows, he was convinced he was protected from the glare of hope that had drawn everyone else to the sunburst weekend. The day creeping along behind the hedge of the city's skyline, he left his office, falling softly to the ground floor. He pushed open the lobby's heavy glass doors and leaned into the canyon winds. All about him scraps of paper flew through shafts of light and beams of darkness, like disorderly flocks of pigeons; and pigeons, whirling like orderly scraps of paper in a maelstrom, turned black then white in the glaring changes. He was alone in the city's deepest place, and still the day taunted him, peeking over his shoulder and flashing a troubled smile.

He avoided the day by sticking to the western walls, his head tilted to the cracked pavement. It was only a few blocks to the hole in the ground where he could glide easily from floor to floor until he found his streetcar. Mostly full on other days at this time, Fliegelman had beat this day's crush by waiting. Taking a spacious seat, he rode underground to the far side of the hills near the ocean, and there the streetcar rose to the surface in his neighborhood still wrapped in calming fog, which, although it had surrendered downtown to day's bright charge, held Fliegelman's neighborhood until he could get to his apartment where night could soothe him and he would have a few hours peace before the weekend's assault.

He fell on his apartment like a soldier on a dead brother. While Friday's afternoon had pulled everyone else out into it and then dragged them further into the evening's whispered promise, Fliegelman resisted, abetted by the darkness. Those going full-out into the afternoon's bayonet light would be transported by the pale glows of evening that imitated daylight. Captured by afternoon's lances, they would find that first light repeated in many variations—in bars, in movies, on bridges, and even in the downtown itself, all gussied up as it got on Friday night, looking like a bad day in an ill-exposed photograph. But Fliegelman had resisted the afternoon's first call by staying behind, and now had enough fortitude to make it through this first short chapter of the weekend. He would be okay for this Friday night, this teasing trailer of the next two days, if he could put off thinking of Saturday and the immeasurable length of the weekend.

He cleaned and forgot. He wiped the dust from the molding that lined the rooms of his apartment. He cleaned his kitchen cupboards, swearing to throw out old canned foods and broken, greasy boxes of spices, but for now arranged them by height. He swept. He cleaned around the packed-up bits of his life that cluttered his apartment. There were little camps of dust on the underside of the knobs to all his drawers and doors, and it seemed several hours eradicating these. He was amazed at the tenacity of things, how even in chaotic entropy the dust bits clung to one another.

While cleaning, music helped push the time down, but only music from the radio, for the radio was company, a voice that spoke to everyone and breathed and clunked in the studio at the same time that Fliegelman peered over the back of his stove and wondered how it got so dirty back there. He forgave the seven-second delay they used on radio because no one ever said anything bad. Records or books or even television might take Fliegelman to memory, might tell him of things that had happened or would happen, but radio kept him there with its insistence on the time; it helped Fliegelman get over the time because it was no other time than now. All that evening he cleaned and listened and forgot.

When there was nothing more to clean, or to alphabetize, or group by color on the fire's mantel, he retired to his chair. He felt he had cleaned so much that he had cleaned the air between his sitting window and the church. Friday's cleaning had left his church exposed, a sharp pang that his conspiracy theory was right. For the moment, however, he was content watching it. It had been hidden for so long. This church, in the Italian style, in marbles of graded hues, had always been a friend to him. It stood on the eastern ridge of hills between Fliegelman's ocean-front neighborhood and bayside downtown, and since he had lived here,

Fliegelman had watched the lights of various days passing over it and turning it first white-yellow, then mint-green, catching reds and purples at sunset. At night, showered with sulfurous lamps, it was alien and comforting, rising above the street's calm and flirting with the sky. Like a river, as with all great buildings, the church was always the same and always different.

An hour passed watching the church. He remembered nothing of the coming weekend. However, as the comforting dread of sleep began to embrace him, he glimpsed the conspiratorial days perched like dark gargoyles on the church's towers. This was where the days would start, and they waited there on the church's hill, greedy for the weekend, pushy and rude. He darkened his apartment and begged for sleep.

When he woke, the room was dark, but it was the gray and brown dark of sashed light. Saturday, weekend's strong man, had come, and his suspicions confirmed themselves. He put his hand near the curtain above his head and felt the radiance. It was sunny. It was warm. It would be hours yet before darkness. Even if he were to try and hold the light away with curtains and blinds, it would be of no avail to his predicament. The light would seep through, as indeed it must have seeped through his east-facing windows, and lay swords of light that would traverse the rooms as the day wore on. He knew it was full light out. There would be no escape. He conceded and opened his apartment to the assault.

He didn't need a clock to know it was still early. The day stood out there, fresh and straight and clear, beaming. Morning had just sprung itself upon the city. Things were quiet, stirring. A streetcar clanged, and three dogs barked. He knew it was a Saturday without consulting either calendar or newsman. He could tell Saturday from Sunday, as well, and any of the weekdays from any of the other days. Who said the makeup of the week was arbitrary? Each day had its inescapable name and place. If somehow Saturday managed to come on a Wednesday, the whole city would collapse on itself, beginning the day with extreme hesitancy, then folding down and down on uncertainty until there was nothing left, a lunacy of improbability like that of the day beginning on the left hand where it had always begun on the right. Lovers would cease to love, and chairs to support. It was possible, Fliegelman admitted, that the days were formed by the way people looked at them, but the insistent Saturday that loomed outside did not accept this theory. It stamped its foot six times and called its own name over and over. This day could be Wednesday only if sea urchins were bank presidents.

He resigned himself and felt the glimmer of morning's cool hope that forever cheated him. His dread took a shower, while he went down to the lobby for his paper, the thanked-god-for paper. Standing in the lobby, he opened the heavy door and felt in a breeze that the day might restrain itself. As he sat to his quiet breakfast of coffee and a roll and dull newsprint, he realized that it was only the quiet of the earliness that led him to hope. In a short time, the day climbing up and up its own wall, preparing to roll onto the boxtop of the city, more noise and more movement were sure to follow, and his hope would dissipate.

Fliegelman feigned the kind of breakfast that those who still possessed their desires would be having. He tilted his chair away from the small table near the window, the chair raked so he could cross his legs nonchalantly, casually, sportily. This angle also brought his torso closer to the table and gave his upper body an intentness that hunching, legs straight under the table, concealed. He appeared, he believed he would, to be zeroing in on the entertainment section spread out before him. What a stunning combination of poses, equal to the day's tasks, both relaxed and intentional. Those who would take on Saturday would need just this pose to become a part of it. Too much laxity, and the day would leave you behind; too much force, however, and the day would balk. No, this was neither a day for seriousness or relaxing. It was a day for serious relaxing.

The newspaper had a few things it wanted to say to him. There was much to do, and much to be a part of. On Saturday news of crises foreign and domestic, distant and local, global and personal, took the day off, and the paper was much more a guide of things to come than what had recently erupted. He skipped the flaccid headlines and went straight to entertainment. The events listed first and biggest were those requiring the largest attendance. Professionals coached sports to come out and be a part of the home team. Spectacular music, good and bad and always loud, played throngs outdoors and in. A run in the park was sure to be more cordial when joined by ten thousand beaming and sweating. Museums painted culture as the choice. And of course, the time to buy was right, now that everyone was out and about and bursting to bustle.

The day was filled to the rim with excitement, filled to overflowing with option. On such a day, such a Saturday, only two things were not advisable, according to the paper's prognosticators—staying home or working. To bolster this opinion, talk had been going on since the end of the last weekend, lamenting the loss of that weekend at Monday's gloomy rise, pushing ahead to Tuesday and Wednesday with pleas to hang on for Friday was sure to come, and Thursday was the next best thing, then Friday with its chanting almost here, almost here. This goading came from every angle, from every medium large and small. Weekend was the inhale and exhale of the week, the simple, unconscious motion that kept the week in circulation.

And here sat Fliegelman, hunched over the prospect, hearing the call, but not heeding it. Hating it instead. Hating the thought that so much time was his own and that other people had so many ways of spending that time.

He closed the paper. He ignored the call. He uncrossed his legs and gave up the pretense that he would join. He stared at breakfast, broken by his desire's departure.

There was a time when he shared these things with his desire. When the weekend came he and his desire were off, joining all the other desires in their desires. As his desire had filled him then, it ate him now, devoured him so much that he could not even remember it. He took the feeling from this dreadful breakfast and applied it to those times, imagining it had all been as horrible as this morning and thinking he had been a fool to let himself be so taken in by his desire. How desire had tricked him so.

The day taunted him, but Fliegelman fought back, and rose from his tired chair to the challenge. He could outfox the day, he figured, for that was the only way with such a bully. He could go out into the day, disguised, and knife

through the day's certainty and pick up the pieces of everyone's desire, the little bits that were sure to be left like gum
wrappers. The day, the conspiracy, and the strength behind
all conspiracies could not hold him. He had broken any
conspiracy's first rule; he had discovered it. This is why the
day now taunted him worse than ever. Its bold front was a
demand that he stay home, and at home hide from the
conspiracy, the regulation of sunny days. These weekends
had haunted him, but he knew their secret. To stay home
was to give in. He could rescue the day from itself. He
could be out in the day and know its nightlike secret and
make himself immune to it.

Grabbing both his shoulders from behind, he kicked
himself forward in triumph and got dressed.

He dressed for the day, so the day wouldn't recognize
him. The day would expect colors of fog and textures of
dark sky from Fliegelman, thinking it had beat him, if the
day expected to see him at all. He would none of it. His was
the edge, so he dug deep into his closet's rustle, rustling up
some clothes of his desire's choice. When he found the suit
of yellow and green, the day's colors of preference, the suit
of soft cottons with the sleeves and pant legs that went
either up or down, the formless, informal, play, jump, and
watch suit, he knew he had scooped the day badly. With his
sneakers to match, he would sneak among the day, among
those out in the day, among the others dressed just so, sneak
and peek his way among the coursing desire, looking ever
so much like those who loved these days, and ever so un-
much like Fliegelman. He was the perfect spy, the unsus-
pectable, his secret of the conspiracy tucked under his arm

like the harmless, quiet newspaper. He could reclaim his desire, bit by bit, microfilming the desires of others right under the nose of the day.

He would beat the day on both counts; he would be of it and above it.

Fliegelman left his apartment with its windows open to the day's challenge and loped down the stairs propped on shaky handrails. The door flew open before him, disclosing the city and his neighborhood.

Fliegelman's city was a great city, peninsular hills bounded by one bay, one strait, one ocean, and connected, it seemed, to the world by two bridges. Like all great cities, it was not one vast face speaking a simple message, but a chorus of neighborhoods, not particularly in harmony or even in rhythm, but coughing a cacophony of catcalls that blended in their dissonance to one fractured but comely song. Fliegelman's neighborhood was a hushed murmur of families and their simple houses. Built on the western slope of the city, built on a sandy descent to the ocean, his neighborhood was even and huge in its babble of street names, yet being in the city still, afforded no room for lawns and their expanses. The buildings here went one, two, three in the air, like Fliegelman's, and were pressed up against one another, like Fliegelman's, and most were divided into one, two, three flat houses each, unlike Fliegelman's, for Fliegelman lived in one of the those buildings that was originally intended for the statistical three families but had been converted to make room for the odd person without family. Six lone people lived in Fliegelman's building's six apartments. Many of the city's neighborhoods were nothing but these smaller sets of rooms, but the beck and call of these neighborhoods was boisterous in the extreme. Fliegelman's neighborhood fell quiet. This is why it was his neighborhood.

Mere blocks from his apartment was the city's great park. By the time the city had earned its need for a great park, the rest of it had filled, growing as it did from the bayside westward, and the only open spaces left were the once uninhabitable sandy dunes where Fliegelman's neighborhood now surfaced. The park was forced to grow mammoth trees and exotic shrubbery, museums and hothouses, playing fields and long paths that led away to corners of the park carefully cultivated to look as wild as the wildest wilderness forests. It was such a feat that it survived, and it still called the citizens to it, as now it called Fliegelman.

He crossed into the park under the guardian gaze of two copper cats gone green perched on granite globes. He saw what he expected on the broad avenues of the park, which were closed now to cars. It had begun, he knew it would be so, this filling of the park, this population of what mostly was solitary. In his office on Friday he had questioned the park, so many fingers seeming to point at it, and the park had whispered some serious allegations about the weekend and the loud days. It had asked to be forgiven, as it was only an accomplice, but Fliegelman could not stay the sentence. The park was a zoo on weekends.

Great swirling groves of eucalyptus made walls in front of him, a mirage of vast solitude urging him forward. He stopped to catch himself. The day was in cahoots here, breezing the trees to lulling peace, when Fliegelman knew no such thing lived in the park today. The park had been captured and could not free itself. This was one of the loutish day's best blinds. Fliegelman benched himself.

From his bench perch, almost exhausted from the day's attempts, Fliegelman knew he did not stand out, and in this disguise was able to draw himself away from the accumulating in the park. Day still sat low on the city's edge, crouched, highlighting half the park.

Those who'd come already to the park were the most eager, the runners and stilted walkers. Some of them, dressed like Fliegelman, whooshed past him on his solid bench, and others, dressed quite unlike Fliegelman, also whooshed past him there. These people were training for the rest of the weekend, keeping their strength for when they knew they would need it most, these most susceptible to the bright day's imperatives. As he watched those on the far side of the avenue and those that crossed directly in front of him and those that trampled through the shrubbery all around him, Fliegelman tried to gauge their urgency from their speed, but from his station he was unable to find their relativity. He would have to run along with them or walk their rapid pace to accurately see who was most driven among them. Yet, it seemed to him that there were those who moved fast, faster, and even fastest, that some hierarchy of objectivity gauged them.

Those who moved the slowest, which was still quite rapid from Fliegelman's seat, wore the plainest clothes, the clothes most like those they would wear at home, jeans or walking shorts, white T-shirts covered by nylon jackets, shoes that made their home anywhere. The next level, the faster ones, were dressed in the main like Fliegelman, in running suit, standard sweat pants and sweatshirts, and their shoes only suited for running and walking. Within this level were levels of color, first plain gray which was plain, then plain pastels, then primaries, then purples that glowed and other colors with suspicious origins, speed ascending. The fastest of all were those in pants and tops made of metal it seemed, streamlined, painted immeasurably close to the body, a second skin of gleaming jet skin that shooed off wind and showed off muscular refinement. The shoes worn by these harriers cost more than everything Fliegelman was wearing, he imagined. Their narrow, quilted soles fit only for high speeds where balance took care of itself and defied falling.

They quick stepped by him, the bulky and the lithe, all seeming fast to him. The red-faced, bulge-eyed, sweating, hoarse-breathed, faltering, and the careless, intent, even granite-faced, all passed him on his bench. The couples, the triples, those followed by companions on bikes and companions on four legs, those who ran alone, plugged into the sounds of someplace else, those who ran alone and begged themselves to stop, those who urged themselves onward as the neurons popped and pain dripped away like sweat, those who high-stepped blank hurdles, those who dragged their feet, those who whooshed and the others who merely wished, all passed by him as he sat there on his bench, and soon the park became a vast blur of blue and gray and pastel and aquamarine and pink hot streaks, nothing but a moving palette of color, a moving palette of chase and search, a movement of bodies that stilled everything else around it, even the swaying trees.

Fliegelman caught his breath. He looked up to the trees

and found their glimmer of leaves so that he might place himself in the park again. Among the swirl of runners, the early ones, he began to see the signs of the others who were filling the park. By their slowness he caught the later ones. They walked in groups and were more intent on one another, it seemed, than on the bands of space in front of them. They lolled, urging their attentions to the bits of park between them. Chattering and chattering, the groups advanced in herky-jerky skittering, like clumps of leaves pushed forward by an erratic breeze, but the random advance was belied by the tensions that banded them together. Some were in groups of five, six, bigger, and some as small as two, couples heads bent on each other.

The first charter bus passed by, the fish-globed tourists dully gazing out at the others who had come to set foot here. It seemed stationary as it glided along the avenue's gray wake. The day cast an odor, sweet, lemony, perhaps verbena.

Fliegelman stood now, cast again. Those in groups had blended with the runners, the runners now thinning, and became part of the color palette that whirled around the stillness of the park and the quiet smooth of the tour bus, as though the tour bus were still itself, though he knew it was moving, and all of the people were a surface to themselves that the turning wheels of the park kept in motion, like a huge conveyor belt.

The day crept slowly up the side of the city, yellowing the park evermore, and Fliegelman felt defeat, unable to keep up with such a morass, this blur of too many people. He had come to track them down, to sneak among them and filter off the loose bits of their urgent desires, but the day's impetuousness, imperative as ever, kept them in such revolution that he was unable to spot them, separate them. Only the statues, of German composers primarily, were immobile. The day breathed down his neck.

He followed the broad avenue to an opening in the park's wall of fir, pine, and other evergreens. This led to the concourse of museums, where he hoped to evade the day for a bit, station himself in front of solid objects and recover enough of himself to carry out his plan.

The concourse was a flat-bottomed bowl walled on three sides by various museums, and on its farthest side by an open concert shell. The bottom of the bowl was filled with seats for the concert's audience, several fountains, and trees manicured flat and broad on their tops. It was impossible to tell what type of trees these were for all their symmetry, row upon row crossed at square-making angles. The first museum was dedicated to the art and times of the civilization that had come from the east to this place, and the second was one that coursed the long travel of those civilizations that had traveled westward from their homes. The third museum, naturally the largest, told the history of the planet, and in it were dioramas of times never seen, animals still alive, and projections of corners of the universe only estimated by imaginary numbers.

The day climbed so insidiously that Fliegelman had hardly noticed, struck as he had been on the bench, how long he and the day had been up. The concourse was filled. Voices and noises rang and ricocheted off the museum walls and earthen slopes of the flat bowl, and especially from the stone band shell where musicians were tuning themselves.

Fliegelman bowed his head and headed straight to the

entrance of one of the museums to escape the day's overwhelming.

Standing in the line for the European museum, he breathed a sigh of relief, for it was as he had expected. The staidness of the line had downshifted the mass that had stunned him minutes ago, and as the line moved out of the day's rays and into the building's shades, he reconnoitered the scene. He would beat this day.

His attention zeroed in on the couple in line in front of him. A man of indeterminate youth and a woman of similar age stood as Fliegelman had often stood with his own desire, side by side and locked onto one another, arms embracing their backs. This couple, he knew, had come here under full sway of the day's hypnotic suggestion.

The lookers one normally saw in the museums in the park, that is during the week's days, when a feigned or minor illness granted such a gift, were not this couple. Those who came during the week were the serious, the lonely, the introspective, and they might even be here today, some of them, but they were not this couple, and they were not the majority on line at the museum today. This couple had come not to see, or for that matter to be seen, though that might be part of their appearance, but to be, to be part of the throng.

What Fliegelman imagined was that this couple were new to one another, and they walked through this day carrying overnight's intimacy. Waking on this day's sharp morn, they discovered, as Fliegelman had discovered, that the day's swift opening and tough promise did not lease the previous night's passion to them, so after a cooing breakfast, they wrapped their desire around them, like the coarse veils of Berber shepherds, and wandered out into the weekend's soft desert. Pushed from night's tent, that tent lit by a thousand candles' promises, they moseyed out in search of what they had almost held last night, not mad enough to stay home and risk the dangerous anger of not knowing one another.

The woman nibbled the man's ear, and he smoothed her buttocks. She laughed at his joke about the paintings of Corot, then looked at the floor's dictionary of tiles for an answer. He agreed with her, quietly vehement, on the beauty of the statues of statuary pots that something or other and this and that, for as Fliegelman's nonchalance bent over to tie his shoelaces, their voices suddenly dropped into a stream of s's and t's and other soft suspirance, alarmed that someone, not necessarily Fliegelman, might try to invade their commerce and steal the commodities of agreement that passed between them. This small talk was as precious to them as desert water.

Fliegelman drew himself back two feet, out of hearing's range and into sight's lines, but his retreat put him in the day's glare and made the couple in the shade impossible to picture.

The line paced up, and the couple was Fliegelman's again. Her hair was a pile of blond strands, pushed up high on her head, revealing the cords of her neck. It was held neatly at the top by an ivory comb, from which a chaos of yellow cascaded. His hair was trimmed, swept away, black. His arm rested now on her shoulders, and he played with a wisp of hair that had escaped the combing upward. Their hair was perfect. The effects they had both achieved, one clean, one unkempt, were both, Fliegelman knew, time consuming. A hair was not in place nor out of it without some design. They had done all of this for each other.

She wore white pants, he blue jeans. She draped a denim sweatshirt, washed well before wearing, and his sweatshirt was white, bearing the fuzzy name and logo of a car. One pair of shoes black with white laces, one white with black trim. What a pair they were. And they had done it for one another, but whether it had happened that their matching was casual and surprising to them, or whether intended and predestined, was not available. It seemed, more likely, a casual intention.

They held one another, the woman looking back at, and perhaps beyond, Fliegelman.

The line moved suddenly and voraciously, prompted by the entrance of a herd of tourists, whose jabbering now moved out of hearing. The couple were next in line. He paid for her, she for him, and they vanished into the soothing dark of the museum's great hall.

Fliegelman rescued three dollars from his wallet and exchanged a curious glance with the woman behind the cash register. The attendant seemed to question Fliegelman's wish to go in, so distracted he must have seemed and so dressed for the light. He looked at her with envy. This was a situation that Fliegelman wanted to avoid, the individual showdown, for it was here that he might get caught by the day, knowing that he stood out up close. But the attendant had the job that Fliegelman most envied. Ignored by the customers as a person, the attendant could watch all the individuals away from the swarm of light and movement and catch their desires like a flu transferred through handling money, or like meaningless bits of change left by forgetful, forward-looking patrons. The attendant took paper for paper and nodded Fliegelman's hurry.

Engulfed by the great hall's darkness, Fliegelman imagined that it was foggy outside, and aided by his recent entrance, almost obliterated the day's harsh optimism.

The great hall was medieval, tapestried. The wall stones and supporting timbers proclaimed true antiquity. Silent knights stood guard in rusty composure. The altar at the far end of the hall, a sign signaled Fliegelman, had been changed since his last visit, this one some hundred years older and deemed, therefore, more valuable. Indeed, it was nicer, he thought, with more hunched gargoyles and pained, wooden saints. The couple had moved off to one corner of the hall where maps of the museum lay in brief stacks. Docents stood by. Children weaved through the hall, escaping, scraping their knees on the marble floor which they thought would slide. A great noise filled the top of the great hall. It was impossible for Fliegelman to break the sound down into its various parts and ascribe the sources. The noise sat like a cloud cover over the hall. Groups formed and went off their various ways.

The couple disappeared. Fliegelman walked quickly from doorway to doorway to doorway of the great hall, looking for them, then to the first doorway again, where he saw the sprouting shower of the woman's blond hair turn a corner above the head of a very short family. He walked quickly down this hallway, past small cases of small coins from a dig in Roman Britain, and turning that corner, found the hair he was looking for, only to find it connected to a head that he was not hunting. The hair stood not with the man he had hoped for either. It was the same hair to be sure. He thought he might ask the person growing this hair if she might not know where the other hair had gone, for it seemed natural she might know, but he realized this was a long shot and went back to the great hall. Crossing the great hall from one of the doorways he had not picked to the other doorway he had not picked, he saw his couple.

He followed them, pacing behind, head bent slightly over a map he had carted away with him.

The couple walked briskly down the corridor, oblivious of Fliegelman, oblivious of the eighteenth-century French paintings of ducks and lobsters and hunting dogs, oblivious of the milling around them.

They turned another corner and entered a hall that was dead-ended, dark and quiet as the dust of dead men. Fliegelman halted in front of a French tea setting, for the couple had stopped at the dark hall's mouth. The woman grabbed the man's wrist and risked a small squeak of amazement. Perhaps she was surprised by the maze's sharp ending or she had been taken by the silence. It was as if she bumped her nose on a glass wall.

Fliegelman passed the couple into the hall of past rulers, knowing as he did that a good following required being in front of the pursued occasionally. He stopped in front of the throne of a fourteenth-century baronial lord. He mustered his wonder and gazed.

The couple began their dance. Here, in the dark hall, Fliegelman's task would be forwarded by the darkness. He watched at will.

The couple slid to the other side of the hall and parked themselves in front of the throne of a man who had died four hundred years earlier. She stood still like hypnotized prey, reverent in front of the relic, while he moved from one side of her to the other, in a swift, sure circle. He bent to one knee, trying to find a detail on the throne's foundation. She quickly moved, turning one way then the other, then sidestepped the kneeling man and glided to the next throne down. The man stood, startled, then moved toward her, casually, his hands held behind his back, slowly, step by step. She inched farther away from him, already looking at the next throne, moving farther and farther into the deep hall. He stopped, held his ground and watched her as she moved away. She had stopped herself. Then the man made his advance, coming on strong and passing her, brushing her back with the inside curve of his arms, stopping finally when they were an arm's length apart and only his fingers touched, not even her shoulder, but perhaps only the material of her sweatshirt. She pirouetted into his arm, and he curled her into his body. They made themselves smaller, squeezing into one another, then dropped their composure, moved away from one another again. They walked side by side, close but not touching, to the far end of the hall. They stopped in front of the splintered throne of a ninth-century leader who might have been a king. Fliegelman watched them from the center of the hall. They both stood looking at the throne. She curtsied to the throne; he bowed. They turned suddenly to one another, facing one another. They stood looking at one another for a long time, their heads pulling together, then they turned, clasped hands and walked straight at Fliegelman, who slipped unnoticed to one side.

As they moved out of the dark hall into the illuminated French art quarters, the crowd of museumgoers Fliegelman had almost forgotten swallowed them, like adoring fans.

Fliegelman kept his pursuit. He watched their dance proceed, as they sashayed around paintings and earthenware, where they dashed in hectic leaving from one another from one side of the room to the other, while they whiled away a few moments in front of a few monuments. Their dance was all leave-taking and reunion, variations only upon these two themes, which seemed to be one theme to Fliegelman.

They danced among the other dancers, the tired old couples, the hopeful new couples, the young who yawned and the seniors who pawed one another fervently. They danced among the troupes of families trouping back and forth like the chorus with serious messages. It was all coming and going.

The museumgoers bent and squinted to read the placards that placed the art within contexts. They looked at the works and recreated them in their talk. Fliegelman was tempted to dismiss the art, but he reconsidered. It had to be here. The dance, it seemed to him, was the product of the museum, but the museum and its goods were the choreographer of the dance. Not one without the other here.

Fliegelman knew the paintings and the blocks and swirls of stone, but they were for looking at another time. He watched the dance instead.

Time wore on, and Fliegelman, sheltered from the day, he thought, hardly noticed its passing until the Brueghel room. Here the couple stopped and sat. The Brueghel room showed ten canvases of the master on loan for two years from their home in Vienna. The room had been refurbished for this occasion with furniture to match that of the home museum. High-backed velour couches, plush, purple, softly suited for colder, bleaker days, filled the center of the room. Heating grates, unused here, separated them. The couple sat and stared at one of the Brueghels, a scene of skaters and cheats, cripples and families, hawkers and animals. It was life in a northern town. It was one of Fliegelman's favorite paintings, not surprisingly, and he was delighted they had chosen it, hoping to find that connection where he had hoped.

Fliegelman came close to the painting, examining the minute figures and moving from one side to the other to keep an eye on the couple's eyes, to gauge their gaze. A look at the couple told him that they had not even seen the painting. Their focus had gone to infinite, and they looked past the painting, to last night perhaps. They had fallen into the sofa because they were exhausted, worn out by their long and controlled dance, by their carry-over of last night's passion.

She spoke suddenly and loudly.

"I know," she said. "Let's go outside. Let's go out and get something to eat or just take a walk or be out in it, you know. Okay?"

And the expected response, the happy reclamation of last night, fueled by the expectancy of the day, disappointed Fliegelman, but he did not grudge them. He had hoped to find their desire and reclaim some of his own, but they held it too tightly. Only the day could pry it from their loving arms.

He let them go, wished them well. He sat on the plush sofa where they had sat and gathered some last residual of their warmth, staring at the Brueghel in front of him, distracted only by the passing of the never-ending dancers.

He left the museum, hoping to face the day down and gain back some of what he had lost before he found it. The day waited.

He stopped, shocked frozen. The day had marshaled itself and the forces of the city. He must have been inside a very long time. No wonder then that the couple had been so tired. The concourse was a bubbling, ebbing, and flowing sea of white T-shirts. Music blared from the band shell. Ten thousand runners had joined for a 10K run and stuffed themselves behind the starting line, dying to start and finish. Bands of blue and white balloons arched over them and the swallowed concourse. T-shirts were the runners' trophies given early, the prize that went to everyone. It was a fun run, proclaimed the shirts. The music stopped. A loudspeaker enjoined the runners to get ready, get set, and they were off, a bobbing, churning mass of runners running the same way, screaming now over the voice of the loudspeaker. The music might have started again.

The day had beat him. The day had seen him go inside and had outside held sway and swayed everyone to join with its stringent demands for recreation. The conspiracy held.

Fliegelman watched the runners. He knew that the park had been cordoned off along with several kilometers of the city's streets. Vans with cameras followed the runners. Fans with cameras followed the runners. The runners themselves held cameras. It was this morning googled. They all ran and ran and ran, an endless running of runners, high-stepping and searching and screaming.

Fliegelman's couple stood next to him, smiling, envious, rejuvenated. They looked at each other again and then began running after the runners, catching up with them and falling into step with their footfalls. They would probably not get a T-shirt, the woman yelled. But they would do it and be there, the man yelled back.

The runners so choked the park's avenues that Fliegelman had to wait for the ten thousand to pass, and that would still be some time, for those in the back of this pack had not even begun to move at all. He sat by the fountain and watched their hopeful faces and their perfect and dumpy and tall and short and well- and ill-clothed running bodies go by. They were all straining to get ahead so they could finish. He could only sit and watch the day's long victory parade.

Fliegelman sat on the edge of the small pond in front of the museum. In the center of the pond was a small island around which swam orange and white speckled carp, and on which sunned a solid and unmoving turtle. Also on the island were two statues. One was of an Ohlone Indian brave, the other of a native mountain lion. The brave knelt on one knee, his bow arched taut, the projected arrow held permanently aimed and ready. The snarling lion crouched, ready to pounce forever. The two figures stood on opposing ends of the island, golden in the day's light, and stood at the ready for one another. Stood there strung and crouched always. Meanwhile the runners ran on, pushed forward by the day's big plans.

Fliegelman went home. Walking back from the park, the day haunted him. Sweat running off his body under his sweat clothes reminded him that he had lost. The day sat on the western edge of the city, hinting that night would soon return, but it sat gloating, whispering in Fliegelman's ear.

Fliegelman made it home and shut his apartment. He leveled the blinds and snapped the curtains and hoped to imitate another type of day, a weekday or a gray day, but this day proved too pervasive. The day filtered in through Fliegelman's fortress, snuck through the backside of his defense. The day's warmth could not be stalled. Fliegelman wilted. He sat down in his chair and sat for hours and watched the day wane and slip away. From his chair he could not see the day easing off into the ocean, for he was turned to evening's approach. As the day's bright smile faded over the city, he saw the first fingers of evening's glove grab the church's hill and begin to pull itself up. At least there would be some respite here, some breaking away until tomorrow's day, twin brother of today, returned.

Hours passed. In this season it took many hours for day to give way to evening, the day stubborn and powerful, not like the days of his desire's season, when night simply stepped in and grabbed the city's reins. Yet Fliegelman hoped surcease. He watched his church and saw the night begin to wash and polish it in hues of comfort.

Finally sleep came to him, but when he woke there was the day again. If only insomnia had pulled him from bed to show him the true night's middle, when day had given away completely. But there was day again, ready to take him on.

He knew that today he faced another failure like yesterday, when he had thought that if he could sneak through the day he might reacquire desire. He had hoped, not to find his old desire, for he knew that was impossible, but to pick up the lost bits and pieces of other people's desires and make for himself a new desire, a ragtag desire of other people's carelessness.

On this next weekend day he had also gone to the park looking for those scraps, but could find nothing there. Perhaps that is why everyone else had been so obedient to the day's reveille. They had all lost their desires and had gone out together to find this desire in the bright promise of the day's magnanimity, but the days had conspired to rob the entire city of its desire. Fliegelman listened to the sound of the city working hard to find its desire, playing and laughing and running and driving and all the other moving and noisy ways it searched, but he heard nothing. Desire had left everyone.

Finally this second hollow day did end. Sunday's night came in from both east and west. The fog rolled in and met the night, and the two mixed, and the city was once again a peaceful city, Fliegelman's city, the soft city of the soft season where Fliegelman could comfort himself and tuck himself away. He left his apartment and took a walk. He knew there must be some way to escape this conspiracy of the days, and he took to the streets to read the solution in the quiet pages of fog that blew past him.

He returned to work the next day and found the day as he had left it before the weekend's clear storm: fog blankets covered everything, and all was business again. His fellow office workers seemed tired from their resting weekend and drooped around him like wilted flowers. Complaints were heard, most regarding this day's dreadful weather and mourning the passing of the weekend's. Fliegelman mentioned nothing of the conspiracy.

He fell back into his rhythm of shuffling and sorting and

subtracting and adding and bringing numbers to accord. True, the exhilaration of the past season's work had left him, but it was the course of things, he felt, and he shuffled himself into this pattern of days and work. Business was slow enough to accommodate, and quick enough to absorb his losses. The weeks went by. Fliegelman pushed them along with walking, nights and weekends walking, constantly walking.

He walked everywhere in the city, through all its quiet neighborhoods and all its loud ones and tall ones and rich and poor ones and the hilly ones and the ones cropped close by the city's three waters, and he read the blank pages of the sheets of fog that crossed his paths and searched for some way to beat the weekend's game.

Then one night, in the thick of the city's shopping district, stock-still and staring into one of the windows where he had once seen his desire changing, he saw vividly a way to outfox the weekend and the cruel conspiracy of the days.

FLIEGELMAN
AT RETAIL

□

He quit his job. That was the first thing. Doting on the weekend's sway, Fliegelman decided that his job was partly at fault for the weekend's flaunting its muscular music over a city devoid of desire. His job was one of those that would not bend to any other wind but its own. His job, it seemed, had been in on the conspiracy, breaching no piracy of the regular Monday through Friday that ate up the intermediate third of the day's precious hours. He considered asking that he be let in during those vacant weekend hours when the tall canyons stilled themselves, but business was a regular guy. Move one paper clip on that hallowed desk, and business would know. You couldn't get away with a thing.

It bothered Fliegelman that his job held him rooted to such a regimen, a law laid down. It was only natural. Why else should the days want to pluck weekends for themselves? Business perhaps was the dark horse behind it all, conning the day with towers of power to serve its own purposes. That was the nice thing about business's bigness: it spent so much time watching for the missing paper clip, and had so many clamoring hopefuls, that he could leave one day without being noticed.

But when he quit, he quit with his own agenda locked carefully away from the prying eyes of the business day's spies. Piecing together what he had garnered of business's culpable capabilities with what he'd read in a shop window's glare, Fliegelman had a plan, a plan so insignificant, so minuscule, tiny and hardly there, that it could not help but sneak through the cracks of the monumental forces that dictated the statutes of his life.

He would work retail instead. Retail was desire, he felt, the customers with their hands on things, the workers letting them have it. He saw desire everywhere in that shop window that gray, superb evening, and saw that desire did not leave the shop in the bags the customers took with them, but that desire lived in the shop. Retail was desire, and when you worked retail you had to work nights and weekends, for that was retail's schedule. Nights and weekends, retold by retail, could save Fliegelman.

When Fliegelman announced his retirement from business there was, as he expected, little alarm, but on the last day of his employment, he received a small party and some gifts. When he came back from his usual lunch of walking, window gazing, and snacking, he found his office festooned. Quavering ribbons hung from his air ducts. His desk had been cleared of papers and filled instead with paper plates and pineapples and sugary goodies, and across his windows hung a banner of printouts matrixed to read page-full letters, GOOD LUCK FLIEGIE. Fellow office mates materialized from behind him and made free with slaps on the back and endearing glances. These were people he had hardly known, and yet they had come out to see him off. He was touched by their farewell and their winking admonitions to come back and still be a part of the gang. It wasn't that he had never liked them, it was only that he rarely saw them, business officiating them into their cubes. Mostly they were men, for men were mostly business. They stood there in their impeccable suits with their impassive smiles. They asked where he was going, and when Fliegelman said retail, they all went on about chains and franchises and warehousing and margin, wishing him well and urging him onward. The talk of high finance, high above the city's streets, was wearing after all, suited as Fliegelman was to leaving. As the snacks were snatched up the mood was lightened and so was the room, as one by one his office mates went back to their offices, last goodbyes in hand. Fliegelman was told he could leave early, as soon as he cleaned up after himself.

In his empty office, Fliegelman stared at the banner with its message. The gray day, only momentarily, only slightly from its shades of gray and soft fogs, let slip through a sinister smile from the building's left side and shafted bright on the glowing good-luck banner. Fliegelman ate the last piece of soft cake on his desk, pensively chewing the white cake and the pale green frosting that tasted of nothing. He cleared out.

In his walks through the city, Fliegelman had taken note of the various kinds of stores he might work at best. Out of question first were the high-price department stores with their lavish displays of lovely goods and the calming escalators. Out also were the smaller boutiques, boot and shoe stores and tailors. Also out were electronics and sporting goods, hectic sellers of leisure goods. Business-supply stores were certainly out. Restaurants were out in the cold, for the work there seemed too rigidly hard for anyone save the very young and gregarious. Liquor stores and grocery stores outweighed themselves by the sheer bulk and perishing nature of their products. What put out all of these stores was simply the single-minded nature of the desires to which they catered. Each spoke to desire, to be sure, but it was either the base desire of food and consumption, or the all-consuming nature of one specific type of desire. What Fliegelman wanted was a store that held all desires in one product, one store that served all to all.

He wanted someplace where the customer could stay for a long time, time enough to act out desire, perhaps, not simply a station for picking up desire's idol and shipping it home in a shopping bag. He had not left business, after all, for such purposes. He was afoot with serious things in mind.

These deductions left him with two options, as far as he could see. There were record stores and there were bookstores. What record stores had going for them was newness, nowness, getting everything as it came available, catching sounds almost before they were made. And everyone bought records. But his hair was not right for this kind of work, and as he strolled the narrow aisles of the record stores, he felt much too old in the presence of the clerks who shrugged off his questions. There was that, too. It seemed protocol that record-store clerks didn't talk much with questioning buyers. He had noticed that he could stay as long as he wanted in record stores without ever rolling out the dough for his disks, and many of his fellow shoppers shopped interminably, but the majority, those with the frenzy of desire dissolved in their smiles, packed their bright yellow bags and begged off staying to listen and look.

So, a bookstore. A bookstore offered so much in desire's way. Fliegelman instantly understood the comfort there of stacks and stacks. There was time enough, certainly, to read whole worlds should you choose. Quiet times and busy times, and time to spend like money to spend. The customers talked, and the clerks talked, and quiet music made time in the background. And this most importantly: an infinity of desires, a vast galaxy of desires, with desires in every shape and color and size and interest, and lots of time to delve into these desires. Standing before the spine-to-spine books displayed in the windows of bookstores, Fliegelman felt the call of desire. Books did not bleep or clang, or fit well or fill you up, make you faster or younger, or erase your sensations, or keep the neighbors up all night. They were nothing but inert paper and ink and desire.

The store he chose was perfect and looking. It was called Sosii Books and Coffee, after the upstart bookseller of Horace. The store's logo was a juvenile in a toga sporting a shoulder-strapped box of books and steaming cups of coffee, as if a vendor at a baseball game. The logo showed white neon in the store's front window and black on white on their bookmarks and paper bags and canvas backpacks.

Many things beckoned Fliegelman here. The coffee bar portion of the store allowed customers a longer respite than those bookstores without pastries and small tables and uncomfortable chairs and the cheap rent of a cup of coffee. Fliegelman had often sat here and watched in the careful way that he watched, heedless of the marble-faced clock. Sitting in the coffee bar, alone among others, Fliegelman noticed that the clerks who worked the bookstore made of the coffee bar their own private kitchen, privy to endless rounds of sustaining food and drink. It seemed like being at home. There was not any sense, really, of the coffee bars of old with their intellectual debates and gatherings of greater and lesser minds. Who would want that now and here? No, this was a place for desire to take a load off, and load up the body with sugar and caffeine and other stimulants.

The workers at the coffee bar offered their own enticements to Fliegelman. They were mostly young, mostly hip and rebellious, with black jackets and black pants and black boots and jet-black and sometimes orange and sometimes green hair. He had wanted, in his designs upon desire, to watch the young especially, for they seemed to have a special rapport with it. It was not that the young held sole rights to desire, nor that the old sold off desire as they grew steadily away from youth, nor necessarily that the old were on top of desire, but the young were restless, and this allowed desire to shine through their shaking attitudes. They had not as yet made compacts with desire, squeezing it into squashed jewels hid under the heavy coats of age. Desire had a field day with the young. The young were just getting to know desire, and they trusted it implicitly.

The bookstore clerks were older than the coffee bar employees, but that was all you could say of them uniformly. They ranged from coffee bar graduates—wearing black still, but styled and coiffed—to those like Fliegelman, refugees of business refusing to take business at its word. He wanted to get to know them all, for he'd overheard that this was not a real job, but one that kept you alive while you wanted to be something else.

Then there was the store itself, the plant of Sosii books, and within the store two things that Fliegelman had hoped for—the inside of store, its decorations and contents, and the outside of the store, its surroundings.

Ah, the painstaking felicity of the store's makeup. The floors were carpeted with dark green, tight-woven plushness. The shelves were light oak, all custom built and varnished, trimmed with the carpet's matching green color in a phony wood. A lot of everything had gone into this plan. The walls were white, but white toned down with some brown and pink hues, so subtly blended as hardly noticeable. Shining white lights tracked across the ceiling. Above all, it smacked of urgency. The books were responsible for that, for this was no used bookstore with its dusty, musty claustrophobia, it was new and very new, exceedingly, excitingly new. The books were crisp, hardly dried from the printer's ink, it seemed to Fliegelman, and they stacked and spined out and faced the customers with regular, perfect, enchanting messages. The yellow and green covers, the subdued purples and academic blacks, the photographs of wilder natures and wild-faced poets, the glittering, raised red letters of horror and romance, the multitude of types of type, the blocky hardcovers, and the smooth, sweet paperbacks. They were all a part of the allure, luring the customers in and around the comforting, endless maze of magazines and cards and calendars and sweatshirts and toys and fuzzy worm bookmarks. A profusion of products, yet each one had a name of its own.

Because of all this urgency, this slow desire just ready to be cracked, the customers were those that Fliegelman wanted to meet, those as vulnerable as he.

There was still more. Sosii Books and Coffee was located centrally in Holiday Plaza, and this was no placid place. Holiday Plaza was part of some newest rage cooked up by city planners. It was part retail, part business, part domicile.

On the ground level of the plaza were the retail shops: Sosii; Harry's, a restaurant where all the waiters were rising writers who copied excerpts from their latest stories and poems and attached them to their menus; the Holiday Four Cinemas, four tiny screens that showed films made outside of the country, where Fliegelman had seen some drizzly movies; Hairnica, an underground hair cuttery and art gallery; Harry's delicatessen; Delicate Harry's, lingerie for men and women; a florist, Thanks a Bunch; a business supply store, Mind Your Own; and Holiday Drugs.

The shops were all like Sosii, new and bright and expectant. In the evenings the shops were a wash of neon-swept glass fronts shot through with white-siren incandescence, all of this outlining the crowds that came and filled the vacancies. The shops squared off the fountain of Holiday Plaza, a bench-ringed fountain of fallen cement slabs that could be walked through, over, and under. Trees sprouted from triangular plots surrounded by flowers trucked in every month from a corner of the agricultural world.

The next two levels of Holiday Plaza were devoted to businesses, fluorescent offices furiously working, mostly lawyers and real estate people.

Above the business and retail levels stood the Holiday's trump card, nineteen stories of luxury modern living. Fliegelman knew it was not a place for those without means as he watched the inhabitants come and go from the elevators there. He had not tried to go up to the top of the Holiday Towers; he had earlier seen the guard who checked in the residents and checked out troublemakers. He could only guess at the opulence of those lives from the fine clothing and distinguished demeanor of the people who did get in.

The excitement of Holiday Plaza was compounded by its highly touted central location. It was deftly located on one of the city's major boulevards with finesse, mere blocks from the City Hall, the museum, the opera, the symphony and the ballet, all these buildings ornately fashioned extravagances. On the other side of the complex buildings was Fliegelman's old haunt, the city's deep canyons of money. The Plaza was, on its other side, at the foot of the shopping district and the finer, tree-lined neighborhoods. All this was to the east and north, and to the west and south were the city's sleeping and bustling other neighborhoods without trees. As the ever-changing sign on the Plaza's busiest corner pointed out, it was the Holiday of a lifetime.

Fliegelman had gone in to Sosii one day when his extended lunch break carried him there with a résumé typed on business's time and machine. The manager wasn't at his desk right now, he heard, and so he spent nearly an hour perusing the rows and rows of books he hoped would someday be his charges. Finally the manager showed up. Fliegelman was dressed in his business suit, and this must have impressed the manager. They sat down right away at a small table in the middle of the children's section.

His résumé was fine. He seemed like a nice person. They needed someone to start in two weeks. But there was the question of money, with which the manager had thought to startle Fliegelman, but there was no question here. Fliegelman knew that retail would pay poorly. It was obvious that a job with such comforts should be so hard-shipped. Fliegelman had always suspected that business made most of its bottom line from retail's front line, and to support that huge pyramid in downtown's canyons, had to cut costs somewhere. Why not the place where the workers had so little to begin with? He had also unknowingly pre-pared for such a cut salary; Fliegelman had saved a lot of money since his desire had left him.

The manager had one last objection, and he danced around it so much that Fliegelman suspected the worst. The job would be nights and weekends, at least to start. Fliegel-man agreed.

"Well, then," said the manager. "I'm Flynn, and I'll be your host here at the wonderful world of retail. Welcome aboard. You won't go anywhere, but you'll have a good time, I'm sure. See you in two weeks."

"Thank you," said Fliegelman, shaking Flynn's hand. "I'm glad to be here. I look forward to it."

Fliegelman looked back as he left the store. He liked Flynn a lot. Business would rather choke than joke about itself. Retail would be good.

Fliegelman untied himself. The ties that bound business only hung up retail. Slacks and jackets gave way to casual clothing, for which Fliegelman would not take the customary business flak. He tailored himself more relaxed in jeans and shirts and sturdy shoes. It only had to be clean. Such strictures felt great falling away. Retail had to bend and lift and stretch and stoop and walk, and if the walking only covered so much ground, repetitious rounds of the same ground chewed up the miles. Business sat and took memos.

Fliegelman's first days were taken up with training, which chugged along admirably. He learned the ropes of the alphabet and the magic of the sectioning of books. He spent most of his time shelving, squeezing authors between one another. He had no problems with the phones and the cash register, and making change felt natural to him. There were other trade tricks that were much like the paper working he was accustomed to, but when all else failed he could put aside paper and arm himself with books, and thus armed, head out for more shelving, acquainting himself with antiquities and the instant contemporary classics. Though all this came as second nature, he kept his nose to the books with the first diligence of all new jobs, and when he looked up, after several days of this training, he found himself at home.

He went on the floor and fell into the rhythm of the retail day. When he arrived at Sosii the store would be slow, taking a breather between the late lunch bunch and the early movie scene. Fliegelman stored his coat, cap, and bag in the staff room and went directly to the bar for a slow cup of coffee in a clear mug. He'd circulate over to the magazines and see what issues had been raised, then over to his favorite bit of the store, the flat tables up front displaying the new eye-catchers. These tables were a mix of all the store's sections, the condensed version of the store, and the store's quickest turns, trundled out in packs of five and ten. After checking on the arrivals and revivals, he went to the main counter and discussed the checkout situation with his fellow employees. He heard all the news, then with a hearty slug of French coffee, he began ringing up his first sales.

Fliegelman answered the phones. He took special orders. He did everything anyone asked him. He served retail well. But he spent most of his shift helping people find their books. Most of the customers knew what they wanted, and he could help these navigate the store, but others were mute in their desires, lacking titles and authors. With these customers Fliegelman knew how to read their silences, matching what he saw in their faces with the books that, at a glance, corresponded. He learned to judge books by their covers.

Nearing midnight, at the end of the shift, he and his fellows began straightening, having worked through two crushes of customers. The store was a mess, all the neat rows and squared tables blurred by the browsing, but within the hour before closing, the bookstore was returned to its morning splendor, all even, and oddly enough, it calmed everyone down, this regathering of solemn order. When last call came, the customers went quietly, except for the last one who knew exactly what book he wanted and where it was. The store was closed, the music turned loud, the money made safe, and they all went home.

Retail's rhythm made all the difference in the world to Fliegelman. He felt a part of the city again, not held high above it in his former office. The store opened its doors and breathed in the fresh and foul airs of the city's waking. There were no closed-door meetings here, everyone met in the open confines of the store. He talked to people and heard their stories; he observed their lives; he listened and began to hear the distant strains of music from long ago. He was learning to separate.

He had restaked his territory. Three nights he worked, and during those days and his two whole days and nights off, he walked the city, assiduous to its calling. Or he stayed in his apartment, locked into foggy security, unpacking little by little the cartons of his life. He had begun to read again. Books borrowed from the store overflowed shelves that had once held only space and dust. Soon the books were gathering on his floor, making his home like his work, which was so much a home to him. The day held true to its collusion with the city, coloring all the weekdays of this season colossally gray and comforting. The unexpected joy of being at home while the rest of the city busied itself was enormous. The downtown canyons and its machinations were hidden from him here, and the evensong of the sea with its bellowing, safe-passage counterpoint drifted to Fliegelman over his quiet neighborhood. Thus was his week defined: home and work and a reconnoitering.

His biggest coup, however, was the manner in which he confounded the weekend. The bright day still led here, charging the citizens out each Saturday and Sunday, relinquishing its power on Sunday night, but Fliegelman had infiltrated these days and filtered out their grasp on him. He stood up to the day, refused to submit to its relaxing interrogatives, and worked on through its harsh commands. He resisted the day by going underground. He spied on the day and learned what it had in store.

He talked. He listened. He unpacked his life. He separated the day's tough canvas into the little bits and stories and faces that he sought. He began to feel himself more.

When the day had held him prisoner, he walked among it a shadow of himself, a cardboard Fliegelman that could be knocked over in a wind slight enough to ripple a poppy's petals. Now he was substantial, and Fliegelman began to remember.

Others helped him flesh out with the stories they told him. He saw people close to him, not as pawns in day's game plan, but as stories of themselves. He heard the concrete memories of their lives, and knew the telling tales of their days. He had rarely spoken with anyone since his desire had departed, and when his desire had been in his life, he had seen little else, so consuming was his desire. Now he was all ears for others. The others he was closest to, whose lives whispered to him and brought the first echoes of his own life back to him, were his fellow booksellers. Each had a story, and as Fliegelman ingrained himself into the woodwork of the bookstore, they unfurled their stories for him and wrapped them around themselves for him to see.

Stories began as gossip always. Small talk was king at the counter while they waited to wait on customers. The more lurid and vivid the story, the shorter time in which it could be told, and as gladdened acquaintance got to know Fliegelman, it was these stories that counted.

Dorianne from the coffee bar was in a bad way with a bad guy named Bill. He wore leather like a decoration for his forays into the city's seamier creases, although he was from a family of rich doctors who lived in the hills across the bay. It was his personal revolution to be so revolting, pumping himself full of nod and shaking his head no damn it no when anyone tried to untie the belts that strapped his arms useless. Dorianne said he was still a good person, and she needed him the way he needed his morphic runaway. She just couldn't shake him, and always went back for one more dose. Small, frail, she still looked the part of youth. Only her hair showed the ravages that should have gouged her eyes and wracked her arms; her hair was blond dyed black, rebleached blond, stiff and lifeless hollow reeds. She had been an exotic dancer for a while, hating its mundane perversion of faceless, gawking men. She had hoped to be a real dancer, barred herself from law school, and shuffled off to a land of dark booths, green and red lights, and dropping quarters. She'd fallen on to the same track as Bill for a while, but those bruises got her booted from Le Voyage du Voyeur, and she came to Sosii for shelter. The money sucked at the coffee bar, to be sure, but she was allowed to wear her dignity there, standing behind the coffee bar in torn, black jeans, a white T-shirt with a black lace bra underneath, an exhibit from her past. She told outrageous stories all the customers liked, took dancing classes from a German at night, and hoped to cut down on seeing Bill.

Fliegelman did not hear this story from Dorianne. He had heard it from Sharilyn. Sharilyn was married and worked part-time behind the book counter with Fliegelman. Sharilyn had moved here from a city far to the south. Her husband had been transferred, his consulting work on the consumption of coffee by third-world countries culminated, and his new job required that he be in this city to help a failing tea manufacturer. Sharilyn had been an English major in school and hoped to teach someday, but for now she worked part-time here, and the rest of the time wholesaling Guatemalan textiles to local import stores. Her husband had picked up the textiles on business trips.

Fliegelman learned all this from Ronin. Ronin told him that Sharilyn was not happy following her husband's vocation. She had been seeing someone else, and Fliegelman knew there was more than eye contact here. She had been seeing, since the transfer, a woman named Beth who bought a lot of her rugs. One day in Beth's office the two had laid down together in a rug's soft folds. Sharilyn hardly ever spoke of it, creating instead a nice fantasy about a perfect husband. She'd told Ronin that she did not leave her husband because she really liked their new house and she was afraid she would unravel on her own.

Ronin also told Fliegelman that Sharilyn had not led a happy life in the thirteenth century, and that was why she cast about so aimlessly now. She had been in the harem of a cruel prince who abused his twenty-three wives. Her only relief then had been in the company of her fellow wives. Ronin said her present behavior was only superbly natural for her, given the facts. Ronin also said that Sharilyn was dark yellow, not a good color.

Ronin's name had been changed beyond his control, but no one knew what his given had been. When he was seventeen he woke to the sound of whale song. That had been his gateway. Since then his search had trekked everywhere. When he was twenty-three he had been picked up by an alien force that had spirited him away to a mountaintop in either Peru or Nepal, and there christened Ronin. Now he lived outside the city, across one of the bridges, in a murky wood, with his lover Greg. From there he had converged on the spirit of a twelfth-century Japanese warrior, who brought him more messages. He was building a business of his own while he worked at Sosii, offering overnight delivery of spiritual aid to the forty-eight contiguous states. Greg was a park ranger.

Ronin told Fliegelman that Fliegelman had cleared swamps in a previous life, and after reading him, refused to divulge his color.

Flynn told Fliegelman about Ronin. Flynn was writing a biography, though still searching a subject.

Gabriella, a law librarian who worked only one day a week and subbed when needed, told him about Flynn. Gabriella took on the job to get away from lawyers.

Zouhair told him about Gabriella. Zouhair had left his family in Beirut to study engineering, but changed his major before each graduation to keep his visa alive. His family moved to Nigeria.

Rose had told him about Zouhair, Quinella about Rose, and Dan about Quinella. So it went those first weeks, the linking of stories, the gathering of the lives. It was not mere gossip that brought the stories to Fliegelman's feet, but curiosity. These were people's lives, and their lives, no matter how scantily clothed, told him about the persons, whispered the names of their desires to him.

After a while the lives spun a web. Flynn had been helping Dorianne to kick her bad boyfriend habit, and this had led to more fine times than either had thought possible. Zouhair had asked out everyone in the bookstore and coffee bar, but they refused, sensing inconvenient marriage traveling with him. Ronin would not work with anyone he had no reading of. Gabriella went every Friday to a pub with Dan, but nothing happened. And on and on, the lives grew together. Retail promoted gathering.

To the web of these stories little bits of Fliegelman's life had begun to cling. The curiosity went both ways.

Fliegelman had been married and divorced, divorced because his desire had come between them, as something always seemed to in a marriage. Desire had thrown them together, and desire had taken them apart, slowly, over many years. His former wife was formal with him, answering his phone calls punctiliously and not answering his letters religiously, excommunicating him from her life. His wife was a dark and beautiful woman, but she had no room for him and his desire in her new, narrow life in a loft over a bakery. She had her own desire to court. After their divorce, his desire had moved in and moved all of his furniture around, reshaping his apartment in desire's fashion, but that only lasted awhile. When his desire moved out, they drifted away from one another, until their calls no longer clicked. Then his desire had left, and here was Fliegelman. His story, he thought, might be tame in comparison to his compatriots' stories, but it was his and it defined him. As he listened to their stories, he began to recall his own, and retelling his story, learned more about it than he had forgotten under desire's mesmerizing gaze.

They listened to his story and sent it around the chain for reaction, no doubt furbishing it there and burnishing it here, but it brought Fliegelman in to this place.

From this smaller web of stories, securely there, Fliegelman branched out and began to take the customers'. These were stories he didn't so much hear as read, in their faces and attitudes and clothing and their requests. There was no concealment on the customer's part, but the roundabout was part of the bargain struck between customer and clerk. They would show Fliegelman lots, but he had to put these lots together. Most customers brought in a pack or purse of an all-purpose kind in which they lugged the goods of their daily life, as if it were life during wartime and they were all displaced populace. Fliegelman saw these sacks as bundles of desire, trundled around in the open for all to see their bulks, but their contents hidden from the naked eye. When customers revealed themselves to Fliegelman, it was as if, suspected of shoplifting, they opened their bags to him and let him peer into them, and Fliegelman, proving trust, stole only one quick glance and looked away, but trying to see in the brief moment all the cluttered bits at the bottom of the sack instead of the stolen book that was not ever there.

Like all bargains this one went both ways, and the customers got something in return when they allowed Fliegelman and the other clerks to look into the dark sacks of their lives. Fliegelman always gave something of their own lives and desires back to the customers, and sticking to the hardstruck bargain, gave it surreptitiously, slipping it to the customer between the pages of a book they browsed or into the paper sacks of purchases they took with them.

It was a great giving and taking, this retail business, and Fliegelman bought whole truckloads of it. For in the giving and taking, he found the little bits of desire he had hoped to squeeze out of the day's conspiracy. Leaving the store late at night, Fliegelman would board the streetcar that took him back to his apartment. On his lap a bag of books and magazines and the bits of desire, all stuffed into that bag. Cresting the hill by his church, he beamed at the thought of so much desire to be had by all, and turning to look back at the heart of the city, he found that desire had not left as he had once thought it had. Desire had dissolved, and he could see now that it covered the city like a fine, shiny dust. He had blown the day's cover.

MIMI'S
APPEARANCE

□

When Fliegelman came into the store the music was changing sides. The needle fell into the groove of blank space at the end of the first side of one of Fliegelman's favorite albums, then the magic of the tape overcame the click stutter, and daring horns came up. It was the same band of steely musicians that played both sides, but there was a difference in the music, a slight change of pace. The first side had been wandering and strange, like angular banjos, but the second side took swift strides immediately and went straight to the end of its four songs with a reckless, unstoppable precision. Though the day's gray face, bluing to evening's change, looked quietly down on Holiday Plaza, the music told the restless story of a fabled sunny land, exotic drinks, and a book of numbers and remedies.

Coffee roasted the air. Fliegelman expressed his way through the line to behind the counter and topped off. It was the slow phase between waves. Under the music people talked, low, secretive, hiding out from where they'd been and where they'd be going. Except at the bar, where low talk always came out loud, the particular forte of the bar hawks who perched there and preached their nonsense loud—the most recent scientific discoveries, political drooling, creative possibilities, relative anarchy in artistic circles, a race of men in the trees. When he'd first started at Sosii, Fliegelman had been fascinated by what these bar hawks squawked, but their staccato squeals soon left him empty. They were vultures who'd carry on to anyone who'd sit still long enough. Mostly they talked among one another, hearing nothing but a space to fill.

He left the bar and went on his introductory route after dropping his coat. Nothing new to note today. Another wonderful another day. The rhythm was steady.

Sosii's counter was raised a few inches off the main floor, the better to see with, centrally parked in the middle of the stacks and tables. Sharilyn drooped there on one elbow, intensely withdrawn. They exchanged one another, Sharilyn suddenly animated after a long sigh. She was leaving for the day.

"It's opera night," she said, and in saying so, cried some full song to Fliegelman. The opera house sat two blocks away, a squat, civil building. It was the scene of the city's most prized occasions. In comparison to the opulent and garish refinement of the operagoers, the staged lives often paled. On the second floor of the opera house was a grand, airy balcony where patrons gathered at intermissions and toasted one another in the chill night's calm. From across the street, in front of city hall's green dome, the best seats of the house, Fliegelman could watch the silhouettes of the operatic crowd, and though from here couldn't actually hear, could almost hear the clinking glasses and the high-pitched, unconcerned laughter. It was a good show.

Opera season had commenced, and opera nights in the

bookstore were festive. The city's favorite color, black, ran rampant. Black was also the young choice, and it was chosen also by the tasteful alienated. Black went with the city's gray days, to be sure, and therefore fit all, and went as well with night's dark schemes. The opera buffs chose black, perhaps, for its signature refinement, but Fliegelman thought that they might also have chosen black for other reasons. The opera house was blank gray stone, but trimmed with gilt, and its interior gilt-laden throughout. Black was regally suited here. Black was also a perfect backdrop for jewelry's gleam. And black was covert, covering the gamut of many indiscretions and allowing for the intrigue of subtle colors to play in its dark hood. Black walked away with this night.

The shift assembled Fliegelman, Ronin, Gabriella, and Rose. They straightened the store while they had their chance. The opera crowd was a flighty bunch. They flipped through the store and overturned everything. They came hours in advance of the show's opening, left only minutes before, then came by afterward again for coffee and desserts. They demanded any purchase be wrapped in a plastic bag, to cut down on rustling.

Finally, after the store had been straightened and the stage for their entrance set, the clerks standing guard, the opera crowd grandly marched in and took their place.

Another fine reason for black was the way it stood out in the bright, cozy shop, sharp and still among the colored variegation of the books and the gleaming lights. The men were in dull same suits, expensively trimmed with white and red scarves, and some wore woolen capes. The women were remarkable in the diversity of their costumes. Black shoes and black stockings, black dresses with black coats, and on these, the accessories to their black matters-of-factness. Shoes were laced with green; stockings spangled with white rhinestones; dresses gave off hues more like scents, so entwined were the colors there; coats were black one second then the next glowed with some dark red or white or gray then turned to black again when the light wind that had exposed the fur's true taint reversed. But it was not simply the range of chameleon colors that drew the conclusion between the men and the women, it was the lines of the women's clothing. They wore gowns that told more than what was seen, not seen. The lines and cuts of their dresses were evasive here, pensive there, tight at waist and cuffs, flowing over shoulders and breasts, daring where they could afford to be. The lithe told no lies in the lines that surrounded them, showing taut and tan skin where shockingly permissible, and those not so lithe wore deceptive fabrications that made whole new bodies.

A man burst into the store, stood squarely in the entrance, his coat pushed open to reveal his white chest. His white scarf quavered. He looked left, then right, then out toward his audience, all of it heroically performed.

"Beatrice," he yelled spectacularly.

The opera crowd was often giddy before the opera's madness.

"Jonathan," came the answer from a woman seated before the fashion section. "What is it?"

She nearly looked horrified.

"Find them," he said, not moving a whit. "We have to go right now. We've been called. Where are they?"

"Jonathan," came a basso voice from the children's section. "We're in here."

"We have to go now. We've been called."

He held his ground near the door.

"Don't be silly, Jonathan. We're not finished here. We've just begun. They will call us again," said the voice, now joined by assents from another voice.

"This is serious. We've got a window table. We won't have the chance again," called Jonathan, beseeching his wife with his eyes and curling his hand in the direction of the children's section.

Three voices called the window word in unison and left to join Jonathan. They all hugged one another on meeting, and four black coats glided triumphantly out into the night which had taken over the world. The other customers and the clerks looked on in a chorus of disbelief.

Two heartbeats and the store got on with its milling. The shades of black still moved about, their production values increased as more and more regular customers joined the throng. This was a pleasing crowd scene.

As the hour drew near, the opera scene made their exits little by little. The store fell into its second hush of the day. There were only a few buffs left. Fliegelman shelved humor.

From his step stool he could see out over the tops of the store's shelves and saw a woman he had not noticed. She stood in the crook between biography and psychology, where there was a narrow window that looked out onto the entrance to the overflowing restaurant and the flowing fountain. Limousines would block her view of the street from here. She clasped a golden handbag to her lips. She wore the usual black. She stood staring, saw Fliegelman from where he stood staring. They both stood there for a long time.

Fliegelman came down from his stool and regrouped at

the counter, hunting for biographies in the always growing stack of books to be shelved. He found three, and two psychology texts as well, and went over to the corner where the woman sat now with a little, brown paperback open in front of her. She was not reading, though, but staring out at the crowd. She wore her gaze like a mask. It was not the impatient one of a late date, nor the angry smirk of the jilted and stranded; it was longing. Her gaze seemed to carry her through the window and across the courtyard and hook into the arms of the black-tied standing there. She was obviously one of the opera crowd, but she looked after them as a true fan who had saved her comic pennies for weeks and months, borrowed the rich employer's wife's gown, and had come up a nickel short of the ticket price. She sought entrance like refuge.

When she looked up at Fliegelman, he saw he was mistaken in his last guess. She was most certainly one of the true opera crowd. Her clothes were not borrowed, and her beauty and composure sang of her status. She looked down at the book and then outward again.

It was her hair that trapped Fliegelman. It was every color hair could be, hard to pin down. Shoulder length and straight, with an elegant, slanted set of bangs, it was brown and black and silver and blond evenly, with a tone of red that showed in turning. He saw that the varied strands also varied in texture, some thinner, some thicker, some frazzled-looking and some composed. It was extraordinary hair. She pulled it behind one ear, revealing a pure gold loop. She stroked her neck lightly and looked up.

"May I help you?" she asked Fliegelman.

"No. I'm supposed to ask you that," he said, turning

away from her, shelving the life of Hemingway between Hoffmann and Horney in psychology, and hoping to enchant her with his nonchalance.

"So," he said standing. "May I help you?"

She smiled at him with jade-green eyes and told him that thanks anyway she had to be going. She shelved the book in front of her, and without looking, grabbed a thick, purple paperback from its niche and went to the front counter. Fliegelman saw that it was the life of Madame de Staël, the most famous woman in Europe. She asked for a plastic bag and left the store.

Fliegelman stood at the narrow window where she had stood and watched her scurrying away. She ran at first toward the opera house, to join the other scurrying couples, then stopped in front of the restaurant. She turned and walked slowly back into the Holiday Plaza, past the orange-and-green-lighted fountain to the apartment house lobby. She turned and stopped, looking back in the direction of the opera, took off her coat, folded it neatly over her arm and went into the lobby, where the elevator opened immediately for her. Fliegelman had seen it all.

He was delighted by his encounter with her, enchanted. Night had pulled his shade completely, and the store fell into another hush that was fine for Fliegelman as it gave him time to ponder her odd movements, her hair and his quick brush touch with her. The hush was broken when the opera buffs returned after their show, though some of them had sneaked back in early, after the intermissions. The coffee bar was full, the forks and glasses clinked, the staff was on edge. It pulled Fliegelman from his standing slumber, this encore of the evening's earlier performance.

He hadn't dreamt of it, but she came back and mingled with the other minglers. When she came in Fliegelman saw her stoop to pick up a dropped program, as if she were tying her shoes, if they did tie, and she now used the program to hold her place in the middle of her life when she closed the book and glanced at Sosii's bar and then her watch. Both glances were rehearsed impatience. She sat at one of the smallest tables in the coffee bar, in the far corner, and read.

The sea of black enhanced the store with a crescendo of jibberish, so pleased were they with the evening's performance. When last call rang, a silence fell and broke their jubilations. The woman in the far corner stood, bagged her romantic life, smoothed herself and left. Fliegelman trailed her outside the bookstore, where she turned away from the Holiday elevators and disappeared around the corner. Fliegelman raced. He saw her as he rounded the corner, where she ducked into a back entrance to the Plaza Building. He raced again, and this time caught her going back into the elevators. When he got back to Sosii the opera crowd had gone on to better things.

The next days harassed him. These weekend days broke so bright and irresistible that the city invaded itself with crowds of lookers and buyers. Sosii was booked from wall to wall, and the coffee bar steamed with company. He couldn't see beyond the end of the line, and she didn't come into his line of vision, but he knew he would see her again. Holiday Plaza, holding so much of the city to its heart, was too small a world to escape without notice, and he did see her again, but not where expectation pointed.

The weekend gave way again, and the soft gray days took over Fliegelman's life. He wanted to go in to work on his two long days off, the hope being he would see her, but he could think of no excuses. So he walked.

He rounded up and down the neighborhoods. The streetcar's silent charge carried him from world to world, through the vast rows of houses to the sharp main streets where the stores did business. He found more churches, but found his still superior in the airiness with which it sat on the hill by his house. He bought a duck from an old man, and pasta from a short, dumpy woman. He came to the city's end three times, each time at vast water. He collected his thoughts and stuffed them in the sack with the duck and the pasta.

At the end of his first day off, he came to his favorite stop on the streetcar's twisting ways, Division Street, down by the strait, between the two bridges. Division Street was up the hill and saw the bay's calm waters sitting under the day's soft sky. Division Street was not exactly Fliegelman's style, but he often came here for coffee at his favorite café, the Café Canetti. The Sosii life had given him a taste for this kind of idleness. Café Canetti was a black, high ceiling with low, black tables. Green columns sprouting dim reading lamps held the whole place together. Here coffee was served as it ought to be, in a cup on a silver tray with a pitcher of cream, a dainty spoon, three sugars cubed, and eight sips of water in a curvaceous glass. It was a big café and almost always empty.

Fliegelman found his table, the one that most suited his approach to this svelte café, empty. He hung his coat, stashed his bags, and pulled out a book. It was a particular book, but that hardly mattered in a café, where reading material of some kind was the basic necessity. He ordered his coffee and Linzertorte from the shy, short waitress who looked as if she knew him without saying it. Fliegelman noticed that others came to cafés to be noticed, called by name, while some came to sit and be invisible. Fliegelman liked it both ways, noticeably invisible.

A book was for two things: to read, and to look as if you read while you scanned. His days off he mostly scanned, but this book shook him by the lapels, commanding his attention, and when he looked up the café had changed, most notably filling with one notable improvement.

She sat here now, two tables toward the door against the other wall, facing Fliegelman, who had no doubts that it was the woman he'd hoped to see. She sat with another woman. The quiet of the café had deceived him, claiming more quiet than was its due, for Fliegelman rarely missed the tricky café comings and goings. This suddenness spilled his coffee when he set his cup down from mid-sip on the saucer rim. She didn't look up.

Her hair, her all-color hair, was pulled back tight. She sat still for a moment, her head down, then looked up with her big, perfect smile, then relaxed that smile away into weighty concern. She looked at the woman across from her, then down, then back at her friend again, the concern still there, though softened and stilled, frankly overridden by her dashing, green eyes. She tilted her hair to one side, staring down at the sugar pot. She talked, and only stopped when the waitress returned with tall, thick coffees and tasteful desserts. She traced circles talking.

Fliegelman stared, but kept his book open at the part. She was not masked black today, having optioned opera's color for the city's flip-side choice. When black would just not do, the city chose, in light of day's gray calm, bright, unreal colors, standing out in them. She wore yellow jeans of a custard hue, a red balloon sweatshirt, and white, rigorous running shoes. Fliegelman had been delighted by her black shades at the bookstore, but realized now that the best color for her could not be so meanly defined. She was all seasons in her tones.

She kept up her silent story and must have been getting to the good part, for she was now bowing across the table to her friend and tapping her own shoulder with three sharp fingers each time she bent forward, each time as if saying "me, me, me." The friend sat hunched, to hear better, it seemed, or to keep her crumbs from the spotless table. She spoke low to her friend. Fliegelman knew this because in a café you could hear the slightest pen roll even over the quiet madness of Mozart or the maddening quiet of "Gucci Pucci." The expressions she used, having moved from concern to concerted, belied any dulcet tones in the whispers she whispered. The hidden microphone might reveal rage or pleading. She upset her coffee with one last gesture, then the story ended, it seemed, or at least the first act. Both women fell away from each other, leaning back in their chairs in intermission. The second part began, lacking act one's gusto, yet inviting intrigue with quiet strains, as Fliegelman strained to hear. He could not.

Her friend talked now. All Fliegelman could see of her friend was her coif and her back, which said FRONT in fuzzy green letters. Her green eyes watched, while her friend talked. The friend divided what she had heard with her hands, pushing half the story to one side, the other half to the other side, then bringing them back together with what

Fliegelman imagined to be pressed palms. The friend tossed off bits of the green-eyed story to both sides, flipping one hand left, the other right, after weighing them carefully. Then her friend tossed the bits of the story back at her, using both hands and tossing them underhandedly. She sat stone-still, looking jaded by her friend's reproachful approach. When her friend finished parceling the story, they both looked down at the table as if it were littered with the tossed-back bits.

Fliegelman waited for the departure of one of them, but the shredded pieces of the story had brought peace instead, it seemed, and both of them pulled books from their bags and settled into reading and refills.

Fliegelman was a little nervous after two refills and an impulsive little tart. He was nervous that he'd have to stay all day to wait them out, the waitress constantly asking to tip the pot. His book, which had so rapt him, he wrapped back around itself and held midair, the sentences now transparent to him as he looked past the book at the woman across from him.

Her friend reached out a near hand and caressed the woman's. She looked up at her friend with her bright smile and put her other hand on top of the two hands already touching. Still holding that first smile, she smiled a little harder and let go. Her friend got up, packed up, and before leaving, bent down. The two women kissed cheeks, lips barely touching skin. Her friend left, and she stayed behind to nurse her last cup of coffee.

She watched her friend leave, then watched the time, while she read a little more and finished her business. Fliegelman could not keep his eyes off hers. One more watchful wrist, and she got up and left Café Canetti, dragging her belongings and Fliegelman's longing stare with her.

The café left Fliegelman. He turned to himself for a few words of consultation, trying to figure out this woman and the forms of her fascinations. Given, she was beautiful. But that was not so remarkable. She was a mystery to Fliegelman, but so were all the other people he saw on the streetcars and in the streets and in the cafés Canetti and K and wherever he went. These were fascinating parts, but they did not add up to the whole whole for him. In the unpredictable way she had acted that opera night in the bookstore, and the manner she spoke with her woman friend today, there was something that spoke to Fliegelman. There was some story here for him, too, but it was garbled by the dark and light shades of her unfathomable hair and the phantom depths of her shallow, green eyes.

Fliegelman left the café and shook the notions that followed him. She was a strange customer, but it was not to be the last of her appearances. In fact, the next was right around the corner.

Fliegelman's streetcar stop, a few blocks down in the middle of Division Street, was in front of the Gym Nopides, where chrome bars glistened, and the walls and windows pulsed from jumping music. You could see everything through the open blinds. Lifters strained. A chorus of clappers ran in place, then stretched and stretched and then three more. It was acknowledged by most to be the hippest place to slim down in the city, enhanced by its Division Street address and its scantily clad clientele who needed it not at all. It was a case of advanced slimming. Only the finest need apply, and only the finest did, beginning slimmers too drowned with apprehension to set foot in these healthy waters. It was a place to be seen while you got ready to be seen in all the old familiar places. Like Sosii, its lucky charms also lay in the plush carpets and total look of newer than tomorrow and better than yesterday. The product here was not, however, in the one-spined books with their thousand faces. Mirrors told the whole story, covering the walls and exposing everything. Gym Nopides was a quiet hymn to perfection.

Fliegelman's streetcar was late, leaving him stranded in front of twenty-six runners aimed at him but getting nowhere. Had the streetcar been on time, he would not have seen her joining the league inside. She warmed up to catch up to them, pulling one knee at a time to her chest and holding the bottom of a white shoe. She twisted and watched, beginning to blush until she looked ready, then fell in step on three and four.

She was much changed from minutes ago. She wore a gray T-shirt over a pink leotard, but no ordinary T-shirt. This was shrunken and pulled, exposing her midriff and the tops of her arms, scooping the story of her neckline, and no ordinary pink leotard top either, but something mined of a rosy ore and fabricated to tell no lies in the tight stretch it pulled on her torso and arms. She wore purple tights the same metal of her leotard, and they showed off the tension of the muscles in her calves and thighs. Her tights flanked her high, covering what the leotard could not, and she wore woolen, pink stockings that would have warmed her legs had they not fallen so carefully around her ankles. She wore much, but hid nothing. Her hair was done up with a pink band. It seemed her hair gave her the freedom to wear anything.

Fliegelman took the stance of the other men who waited for their streetcars gladly, watching in the windows, hands on chins, as if serious about an investment in this scheme. The running, jumping, twisting herd inside the gym were mindless of anyone watching, exerting themselves to pain with closed eyes. The perfect subject for watching was the subject who wanted to be watched unawares, who feigned ignorance of watchers, while the aerobicists feigned their ignorance blissfully, sweating, bulging, flattening, and glistening. All but one, as they bent and jiggled. It was she. She moved along with them, but she kept her eyes open, even when they were down-facing she was wide green-eyed upwards.

Fliegelman's streetcar hissed at him, and he snaked his way among the crowded front to the very back to find a window seat on the right side. She and the gym grew distant and disappeared as the streetcar crawled up the first block then turned onto the slow descent away from Division Street and its opulents.

The next day Fliegelman considered he had moved out of her sphere, his rounds of the city taking him to the poorer neighborhoods. His first stop was the innermost and most colorful neighborhood of the city. The long blocks of the Dolores were lined with sad shops in happy tones, selling everything at cut rates to its family of neighbors because they still owned their own neighborhood here and had yet to be conquered by the toppling powers of downtown's incorporeal business. Fliegelman liked the rumble of this neighborhood, so run down by others but so decorative with its annual funereal processions. The smells of hot foods, the dangling paper men, the red, white, and green standards all laid their ancient claims.

He saw her here in a used clothing store, where they sold clothes by the pound. She was dressed in a fashionable destitution, like many of the city's artists, wearing clothes from the first bad movies in living color. She wore pointy, black sunglasses that hid her eyes, but her hair gave her away. Fliegelman saw her just as she was leaving with a load of clothes three bags full. She was on the streetcar and fading before Fliegelman could make it to the door.

Later that day, the day still holding its true promise of gray, he saw her again, in the old cannery neighborhood that was now stocked with galleries. He had come here to see an exhibition of sculptures done completely with burnt sandwich bags. The exhibition was called "Fried Glad Lunch." He had been told it was a must by a bookstore customer, who had explained the dynamics of the juxtapositions to him, but he smelled something fishy when he got to the gallery, which was an old diner kitchen. The customer had told him to read the context carefully, but the curator had run out of catalogues.

She was not there, but she was across the street, and through two windows Fliegelman saw her. She was at the Peanut Gallery, judging the context, he imagined. When he first saw her in the gallery he took one step forward then two steps back, because he thought she was a statue of herself. She squatted against one wall, watching two people install a huge painting on the far wall. The painting was a field of black. The Galley Gallery owner told him it would sell for six figures. She wore white blossoming clothes, the pants tucked into white boots. It seemed shimmering silk, the blank canvas that draped her. From where he saw her, Fliegelman almost thought she was directing the installation. She watched the artists hang the picture high, as it should have been. Then she talked long with one of the artists, a paint-splashed man with whitewashed hair. She gave him a check and loaded a long brown-paper parcel into the car and drove away.

Fliegelman saw her three more times that second day. Once before dinner, going into a jewelry store, once at dinner in a dark diner where she took the food to go, and once after dinner only blocks from his apartment. He was walking in his neighborhood's productive produce area, watching the Asian women carry their big packages. He saw her go into an ice cream shop. She was dressed here, as she had been on all the occasions he had seen her, differently. Tonight's dress was simple jeans, a pastel sweatshirt, and a big sack purse. Trios of teenage girls surrounded her where she sat at her booth alone, eating pie, ice cream, a milk shake, and drinking coffee. Fliegelman watched her from across the street until a streetcar stopped in front of him and pulled away, leaving the ice cream shop strangely empty.

It was a small city, no doubt, set on its insular peninsula, and Fliegelman had two or three people he often ran into regularly, but this was something more than mere serendipity. Her appearances were deceiving to him. He went home and slept.

He stayed rooted to his apartment the early part of the next day before work. He reckoned his sightings of her and judged them as pure chance, but found this beyond redemption. Something was afoot here.

When he got to work it was its same old self, selling and buying. The store's great rhythm soothed him.

After his first break he went to the counter, registering

all the sales, charging the customers, tallying their desires. He leaned over at one point to retrieve some stray charges, and when he came back up, she was standing there with a book in her hand, her checkbook, and her perfect smile, hair, and eyes. Fliegelman saw close up the lines in the corners of her eyes and the deep nature of her tan, which was not her own skin color. He saw that she was made up with base lightly, a hint of rouge, and a dark lipstick. She wore nothing on her eyes.

She looked at him with all her light, but there was no recognition of him tinting her look. She was dressed in rough tweed over a peach blouse and green cords. She pushed two books for Fliegelman to ring up. She was buying another biography, this of five women in Victorian marriages, and a book of short stories about adultery by a Czech.

Fliegelman rang the books up and out, bagged them and turned them over, while she wrote out a check with a heavy, golden pen. He could not tell how old she was. Like her hair, she seemed to be all things at once.

She pushed the check at him, and he asked for the rectangular plastics that would tell him more than anyone needed to know, but not enough here. She put down her driver's license and a credit card that had a hologram of an airborne dollar sign on it. He copied the credit number faster than his eye could see, then slowed on her driver's license. Her name was Mimi Surbain. She was five feet four inches and weighed one hundred and fifteen pounds. Her hair color was given as brown, but the picture showed her hair as it was. She lived at 816 Holiday Plaza and had to wear corrective lenses. She was born in nineteen and . . .

She took the license back and put it away. You had to be fast with a license.

She thanked Fliegelman, and he thanked her even more. She dropped her books into a bigger sack, looked up once at Fliegelman, smiled and left. Mimi started to leave, then turned around again and came back to the counter.

"Excuse me," she said to him. "You seem to know something. I was wondering if I could talk to you sometime."

"Certainly," he said, and the rest of the night played easy on him.

Mimi had fixed him, held him. Her request to speak with him, he felt, was aimed at books, what she referred to as the thing he knew. Below that simple declaration he saw a thousand lines of fine print that might constitute any number of undocumentable possibilities. She might have seen him seeing her and scored Fliegelman a menace, not knowing that Fliegelman had been nonplussed by their encounters. In this case, her retort would certainly be one of evicting Fliegelman from her life, getting him off her case, and given the evidence, he would be hard-pressed to sway her otherwise. Or she may have seen Fliegelman for the first time when she bought her books from him, and been sold on him from that thirteen-dollar paper exchange. But she was too keen, he felt, not to have seen him before, and too engrossed on some occasions to have seen him at all. The null point of these graphic possibilities was that she had said what she said on impulse, not meaning to ever return and speak to him, as if she were giving him a tip of another sort, for moneyed tips were out of the question in retail. Fliegelman had seen this before, some distracted customer making a minor overture to one of the book clerks, as a way of making everyone feel better after the customer's long day. He was sure that her reasoning to ask him for some sound advice floated along this spectrum, as yet an imaginary number.

His attraction to her, though hardly imaginary, was still illusory, and floated between many points he couldn't quite pin down. Her beauty, he knew, was not something to be overlooked, although he had already discounted that as far as he could, for her beauty was quite common in beauty's commonest terms, and it was quite the chameleon, not something to paint a picture of for lack of the right shades. Her beauty still beguiled him, however, and colored each of her other attractions. What attracted him most had something to do with her desire, what Fliegelman made of her desire in his fleeting glances of her.

Mimi was always at some point of desire when he saw her, but not completely wrapped up in that desire, though she dressed the part. She always stood a tad aloof of those completely folded in their desires, as if she showed up late on purpose to warm up to it and watch those engaged in heated desire. She was encircled, he felt, in a Venn diagram of desire, part but not all of watching, intersecting part but not all of desire. She had seemed to be everywhere at once, and Fliegelman now felt that she stood in at least two places, contradicting all laws. Who could live like that for long?

Having lost his own desire, he was fascinated to see someone else pursuing their own so halfheartedly, half mindfully. This was how she had drawn him, by refusing to lock in step to the heated march, and yet not pulling herself out of the running. She desired desire.

He retraced her movements around the city and retrieved the obvious bits of her desire, but these were only the incomplete borders of the puzzle, the jagged pieces of the even blue sky in the background of her picture. If she would come back and ask him about the thing that he knew, he might find her puzzle's other pieces and piece together the rest of her portrait, the important center of the portrait that was glimpsed incontrovertibly in the dark and light hues of her hair.

She did come back to Sosii, and they did talk books. She would come to see him before the dinner lull or during the last hushed hour of the night. At first she questioned him on authors, gauging his authority. She was especially interested in the Czech author she had bought from Fliegelman that fateful night, and dumb luck pulled itself out of its own top hat again, for Fliegelman had read all of his books on laughter and forgetting, the topics that seemed to be at the top of Mimi's list. There was something about the Eastern Europeans, their optimism among secret policing, that intrigued her. She wanted to read more of them, so Fliegelman drafted her a list.

They went through the entire fiction section together, Fliegelman warding off the stares of his fellow clerks while he gave himself over to this mammoth task. He noticed Mimi's inclination to other foreign fictions and took her through a geography of places from Afghanistan to Zaire. The world of these writers was an endless universe, and she stamped them all in her engagement book on the customary page, taking home one or two each time they talked. Fliegelman knew she was a serious reader, not stuffing fluff or collecting cocktail titles. She devoured other worlds.

When they came to the end of fiction, Mimi feigned interest in the store's other sections, but the only section outside of fiction she could live with was biography. Here she had Fliegelman beat and gave him a few lessons. They had just about talked books out.

The time had come to speak of other things. From the first day she had come back and asked Fliegelman about the Czech writer, he knew that he was right in assuming she had not come back to see him for book chat. Yes, the books were one chapter in this new friendship, but that was not the end of the story.

Where they were to begin, Fliegelman had no answer; it was Mimi who had posed the question. Fliegelman had plenty of questions of his own for her, but their joining had been punctuated by her exclamations, marked by her corrections. Weeks had gone by since they had begun their dialogue, and Fliegelman sensed that time and matter were running short. He waited for some new apostrophe of Mimi's to speak to him.

It came suddenly, when one night Mimi asked him when he got his break, suggesting that maybe she could meet him then, and they could sit down and get to know each other better, flesh out each other's lives, as she put it. This made him a little nervous. There were no breaks in the bookstore, he told her, only dinners and lunches, and he usually got his dinner at eight. It was a date.

She came back three hours later, overdressed for a bookstore dinner. She wore sharp black pants, a black sweater, a string of white pearls, and the smile, hair, and eyes Fliegelman was coming to know so well. She carried nothing but her keys.

They danced between streetcars across the broad avenue and sat at a round table in the back of some cheesy, corporate pizza parlor. Fliegelman suggested it because it was always slow here, no customers, and he always got his food fast because he only had an hour, tops. It was a great combination. She was delighted.

The conversation popped up books immediately, but that was to be expected. The forthcoming change Fliegelman had felt was in order could be received so quickly, just by crossing the street. They ran down the list of the best books steaming fresh out of their cartons, and Mimi told him about her delving into the work of one of Fliegelman's suggestions. The pizza called its number, and they ate for a while in silence. Fliegelman still could not apportion her age correctly.

Fliegelman showed Mimi the pizza-palace napkins' secret passage. The logo here was three heraldic shields, but the stripes showed a coded message when you traced them, and the shields spelled out F-U-N. She followed him easily.

"You know," she said. "You're right. It's just right there, in almost plain view."

That was the keystone that opened the entrance Mimi had been looking for. She amazed him with the path she took from this simple ad vertigo to telling him about her wanderings through the city, and from there to some secret chamber that Fliegelman thought she herself might not even know about.

She raved about the ad's execution, then ranted about the ad's insidiousness, then granted they were one and the same. She tagged on to the corporate idea of fun, hoping to expose it, make it cry uncle as she tried to bring home some truer, less calculated idea of fun, but in the end had to concede herself. She guessed that the ads were not some schoolyard bully that made us follow after this fun, but that we really thought this was some kind of fun we truly wanted, this capital fun that the ads were so bold as to print. It was hard to say, she stated simply, which came first, the need for fun or the funny need the advertisers filled. She took this city for instance, what she called their city. Such hard work, so much fun, and so much work to find fun. Downtown, in those golden office towers, people slaved all day to do what these pizza people had done, get people in the mood for what they were selling by convincing them that what they were selling was fun. Even eggs could be fun, if you gave these guys enough rope. Then, she went on, when those golden office boys and girls got out, they went out into this city to find for themselves what they had been trying to get everybody else to search for, great golden, big-time fun, capitalized and lighted and picked off the heavy boughs of this seemingly endless garden. Look around, she told Fliegelman. Look at this city. These people were dying to have fun. What Fliegelman had pointed out was only a napkin, nothing more, and she insisted that people didn't have to listen to it. She insisted that they could wipe their mouths with the napkin and that no napkin could make them do what she saw them doing. She knew. She had seen a lot in this city. There was something going on here more powerful than this napkin, but the napkin had something to do with it. It wasn't the old chicken-egg controversy anymore. It was more like a chicken and egg salad sandwich. This city was a mess.

Fliegelman took none of this with a grain of salt. He knew what she was talking about and knew that she would get around to what she really wanted to say soon, to what he wanted to hear.

This city. She had gone underground, she told Fliegelman. She had seen things for herself. She told him about the gym and the stores and the galleries and the cafés. She had seen people there not just having fun, but, and she said this again, she swore they were dying to have it, and the oddest thing of all was that they did not look to her like they were having fun. They looked exhausted from all this fun. It wasn't funny.

She stopped and looked up at Fliegelman with her bright, green eyes. He told her that he knew, and he knew that she knew that he really knew. But he waited for her there, for she still had other things to tell him, other things he waited to hear.

She told him she wanted to be a part of it herself. She wanted to want what they all wanted so badly. She had spent too much time in her life thinking she had everything she wanted. She wanted to want more. She watched them and tried to ape their wanting. It had been going on for some time now. She would show him sometime. Did he know what she meant?

He told her about his seeing her, how he had seen her that first night in the bookstore, when she'd dressed in the rigorous black and captured him there. He told her of the next several days when he'd hoped to see her again but didn't, and then suddenly seeing a deluge of her, unmistakably and unaccountably. He told her that he suspected something of the sort when she had asked him if he knew something. He began to tell the story of his own desire, but everything came up short, for the hour had surpassed itself, and he would have to hurry now if he was going to be in time to be reasonably late.

"Fliegelman," she said. "Will you come to my apartment next week? I want to keep this up with you. I still think you know something."

They left the pizza parlor and hurried across the now barren avenue, looking down it at the bright parade of lights. The night snuck up behind them and put its arms around them both.

Mimi's Kempt World

□

The Holiday Plaza Towers spired over the city, but no dreaming spires. The twin els rose to their sheer heights in cold, garish, blocky floors of stone. The architect's designing hands had hoped to imitate some Florentine lightness by adding red marble trims, and some jet age with light tubular railings, but the city's movers and shakers grounded airiness with strictures on such building fancies. The building had to stand up to a rigid scale. The city had fallen seven times in its brief history, and had to shelter itself. Despite these faults, the building stood out. Here, in the city's heart's core, Holiday Plaza was a building everyone looked up to, both for its attempt at cloud busting and the ineffable combinations of retail, business, and domestic desires.

Fliegelman knew the retail floor so well from Sosii, and the business level so-so from running errands to secretaries whose sobbing bosses couldn't wait for certain books with excellent business titles. But he had never been upstairs.

Security at Holiday's lobby was immense. A big guy in a blue uniform was stationed in the lobby, suggesting passively with his sheer bulk the possibility of serious physical harm. There were also the cameras outside the resident entrances that watched with dull red eyes all that happened nearby and told their simple stories to the guard watching five televisions. Fliegelman had seen many people escorted on their merry way. It was a place that invited invitations only.

Fliegelman appeared before the big man in the blue suit. He had spent much of the morning dressing for these parts. His closet had showed him a rack of tortuous business suits and begged him certain questions as to the propriety of his apparel, religiously assuming that Fliegelman wanted a formal statement, but he staved off these inquisitions. His closet was misguided. Fliegelman did want something more than the run-of-the-mill work casual; he wanted heightened casual. His audience with Mimi and her apartment was a step above his normal appearance, but to achieve the business look would be degrading. The business suits from his lifeless past hung like corpses in his closet. He chose instead some big black pants with a big black shirt, shrouded these with a big black jacket, and strung himself dandy with the heretical bolo tie, black and white braided, and noosed by the cornice of an ancient building. He had to look sharp because the dull security guard could spot an imposter. Holiday Plaza didn't take the common traffic.

When he announced himself, the guard didn't blink. Fliegelman thought that it must have been the decorative chip between his shoulders that fooled the guard and paved his way. He was suddenly, in the guard's words, a Mr. Fliegelman to see Ms. Surbain.

The lobby was appointed splendidly. Plush was the key word. The carpets, oriental, and the sofas and chairs, mock deco, were things you could fall back on and sink into. Even the huge, golden Grecian urns, formulated for decorum, looked soft enough to sleep on. The wallpaper was thick enough for a blind man to read.

The elevator rang for him, and he obligingly stepped in. This cubic room was a hall of mirrors. Even the ceiling looked back at him familiarly. Fliegelman had always had bad luck with mirrors, and he reflected that this was probably because he didn't like the look of them. There were too many Fliegelmans in here with him. So, to keep his mind off the mirrors, and tardy himself, for he was always early, he pressed each of the twenty-three floor buttons. Mimi lived on top.

Each floor was different. The second floor aped some jungle scenes, the third was an Aztec camera, the fourth floor flew to Rio, the fifth swam in an island of Parisian lights, the sixth beheld the splendors of Rome, up and up, until the designers seemed to gasp for air, and gave up simple settings to move on to more refined tastes, indulging in styles and nuances. As the elevator neared the top floors, Fliegelman noticed that the hallways grew more and more expensive and impressionistic, seeming to reserve these subtleties for those who could afford the higher elevations where the apartments were the priciest. He also noted that for all the decorative changes in the hallways, they were all basically the same units overlaid with various finishing touches of paint, carpet, lamp fixtures, the obligatory table and its corresponding fluorescence. They paid for amenities and, he imagined, the view from here which he could not yet see. He also noticed no one coming or leaving the apartments and was never joined on the elevator.

Mimi's top floor opened before him. It was the one Fliegelman had expected to see on his arrival, the one most suited to the city's tastes and what he knew now were the astronomical prices of these places. The carpet was soft black, of course, with hidden silver strands like an executive's temples, and the walls were gray, washed with some sloppy black and blue sponge. The fluted lamp fixtures whispered, and the hall tables gleamed gray that had been brushed white. The thinnest mauve trim, pencil-lead thin, divided the gray walls from the flat black baseboards. Bunches of birds of paradise, burnished coal black-blue, flew out of dull silver vases. Only the hidden camera's Rudolph red light threw the scheme for a loop. Fliegelman's favorite days and nights, the foggy, soft ones and the quiet colors that lived in them, had been captured here and scaled down to indoor proportions. The hallway was as seamless as his days.

He had Mimi's number, 2304. He knocked as quietly as he could, for the rich decor warranted a judicial quiet.

He heard nothing for some great long time, then without a warning at all, no shuffling footsteps, no muffled calls from the back of the apartment, Mimi opened the door, the door itself as quiet as a mouse. From behind her the day's anonymous sky peeked through squeaky clean windows.

"Fliegelman," she said, standing close to him. "Come in. This is where we live."

She was dressed in grays, a woolen skirt and blouse with leather boots. The green of her eyes shone out like the sweet, sharp green of the city's lawns during the first rains of that long gone season. Silver jangled on her wrists.

She ushered him in, taking his elbow and coat. Though

he had heard nothing before she opened the door, Fliegelman would have bet that she had been running; she was
flushed and short-winded. She said here, pointing to a bil-
lowing, grège chair, and asked him to wait a few minutes
if he didn't mind, then shut herself behind a dark door.

Perhaps Mimi had done it all, thought Fliegelman, done
the hallway and the apartment, too. Or perhaps the apartment had come this way, part of the plan, or even again,
Mimi might have drawn the apartment with serendipity
before she'd even seen the hall. Among these perhapses,
the one perhaps that never intruded was the one that said
some other person might have decorated; the apartment's
interior decoration bore Mimi's ID without any doubt. It
was perfect in its arrangement and color coordinations. It
lifted itself not from the standard brand of most apartments
with their heroic struggles between decor and entropy, but
from some other magazine. You would have to live this far
above it all to be as sedate and gorgeous as this. The apartment's adornment alluded to some hired helping hands that
combed and kept it so superior, but it was impossible to be
certain on the grounds of its kemptness. Mimi probably did
do it all.

As he sank into the cool chair, he began to see the things
that created the perfect ambience. The big room that Fliegelman sat in—and it was a huge, big room, bigger by two
than Fliegelman's railroad car of compartments—focused
on the fireplace, pointed with its wall's big fingers to the
fireplace. It was the layout of the room that aided this, he
thought, yet the fireplace might have avoided the stares had
it not been for what hung over it. What hung over the black
marble inlaid fire's mantel did not have to coax Fliegelman

out of the comfy chair. It more picked him up and magnetized him to it, and zeroed him in to the black sentence on its appeal. It said, This is not a bitchin' pink surfboard. It was a pink surfboard, life-size and hung sideways over the austere fireplace. It was more than pink, too. It emanated pink, which had something to do with the room.

"I'm coming," Mimi called from the other room. "Look around, make yourself at home. Get a drink, or I'll get one for you."

How Mimi had done it, Fliegelman was not quite sure, but she had made this pink surfboard appear as if it were the only object that might possibly occur here. She had made it so the center of the apartment, that it might have been an alternative altarpiece. Mesmerize me, Mimi, Fliegelman sort of hummed.

The surfboard loosed its hold on Fliegelman, gave way to the other things in the room. The room delicately showed off. The objects that made up its spaces were all quite precious, he saw, gathered from distant places, and what Mimi had done in her collections was to coordinate every thing's color with the apartment's. A certain style of painting, for instance, might seem to clash in style, going by the books, with the tribal relic below it, but the contemporary lines of the disjointed purple and blue-green headless swimmer was forced by Mimi's adroit juxtaposition into an unbreakable orbit with a pink, black-spotted hyena howling on the table just below the painting, howling as if the swimmer were the hyena's only bright moon. The value of each object then was twofold, its value in and of itself, and its value in and around the apartment, doubly precious. The room was content with itself.

Fliegelman went over to the far window
ramic view. Under the gray day's beneficen
saw to the east the city's business canyons, to
church and hill that he saw from his far apart
the south the city's rolling neighborhood
churches' spires. Below him the Plaza players
courtyard to and fro, entering the shops and e
cartoon chase through a house with many roor
the confines of the Holiday's retail floor, cars
parking places and streetcars roped people in. T
hard at work. He was trying to take it all in as
possible, the apartment and its environs, to learn s
more of Mimi's scale and to be able to concentra
odd song she would undoubtedly sing for him to

He picked up and tried to decipher some chip
standing gameboard. Mimi came in, or rather was i
ing close to him already, another soundless appro

"It's a crystalline set of dominoes," she said. '
not really crystalline. Sort of domino-like, but not i

She had changed. Now she wore the clothes sl
been wearing when Fliegelman was surprised by her
door, only in a different color, a muted pink, even the
were the same but of a different color. She still jangled
wrists full of bracelets, which had remained oddly siler
her approaches.

"This," she said, turning away from Fliegelman, '
mystical sphere. It's direct from Lhasa."

She turned the sphere over in her hands, then turr
it over to Fliegelman.

"What do you think?" she asked him.

"It's marvelous," he said, looking at the sphere. "It's a

hough you can see a whole world reflected in this one tiny
place."

"Not that," she said. "Our apartment, where we live."

"That, too," said Fliegelman.

"Come on, then," taking his arm again. "*Le tour grand.*"

The entire apartment was several bits too much, each
room as perfect as the next, and as in tune with the others
as the living room had been with the outer hallway. There
were endless rooms that seemed to have no purpose, and
Mimi left them so. One room was called the study, but it
looked much like the other rooms that had no names. The
bathroom was as large as Fliegelman's bedroom. The
shower could have stood six or seven people, he guessed,
not including the bathtub, which was bigger than Fliegelman's big bed. The whole bathroom was tiled and chromed
to perfection.

The bedroom was the last stop before the kitchen,
which was the last stop. The only imperfection in this room
was the asymmetrical appearance of one of the two matching nightstands, which Fliegelman guessed to be Mimi's.
The nightstand in itself was all well and lovely, but it was
a clutter of things on top, mostly books, and mostly books
that Fliegelman recognized.

Above her bed hung a superb, catching painting by the
artist of the swimmer. This was the grail, and it showed
another headless body, this time floating in a space of special hues, and it floated near a pair of rings, the rings as big
as the floating body. The rings were both spinning, and
spinning from one common axis though their opposing
zeniths pointed away from each other. The rings were a
bright, glowing, almost turquoise color, and they fell in and

out of the picture and changed the direction of their spins and were almost impossible for the viewer to grasp. When Fliegelman raved about the painting, Mimi beamed back at it and said nothing.

Halting the tour briefly, Mimi stopped them in her living room to show Fliegelman something she'd forgot. What appeared to be a sectioned wall moved itself out of the way in pieces to reveal an array of books, records, tapes, and audio and video equipment.

In the kitchen Fliegelman sat at the table while Mimi made coffee for them. Coffee was part of their bookstore meetings.

The kitchen was dry and clean and seemed to have no use for the regular mess that came with such a place. Entropy was definitely on hold here.

Fliegelman went on about the apartment and its appurtenances. Mimi had to agree with him. It was quite a catch. She had decorated it herself. She was glad Fliegelman was so pleased. It was big and worth every pretty penny of it.

"We were unsure at first," she said. "But now it makes perfect sense. We always loved the city, but it could be so hard. We looked for months and months and even lived in a hotel for a while, but it was worth the wait. We've only been here a few months, but it seems like forever. We don't really know how we lived outside the city for so long, as much time as we spent in the city, but we can see that that was another life we were living. We really think it's perfect, but still, somehow, I don't know, because it really is perfect, isn't it?"

Fliegelman assented as a silence broke in. They sat and

sipped. Fliegelman put his questions about the anonymous "we" under his coffee cup and pushed them to one side. Her coffee was better than Sosii's.

Fliegelman shooed the silence away with a catalogue of phrases about the amenable apartment and the lush, contemporary decor. Mimi scanned the strand below, two-handing the coffee. Little by little she interrupted Fliegelman, obstensibly commenting on what he was redescribing for her of her suite's goods, but beginning to draw the lines between what he said and what she was going to say, which was what Fliegelman had been waiting for all along. He remembered that she had asked him here because she wanted him to tell her something, and he agreed with her that he did have something to say, but he knew that she had not finished her chorus yet and he could not begin his refrained variation until she did.

The apartment was the crux of the matter. Yes, yes, yes, she affirmed what he said, yes this and that, and that was where that came from when they had given up that, but that didn't mean anything really because what she really wanted to do was this and had been unable to find anything because what she really wanted was to be able to talk to someone about it. That was when Fliegelman came in, someone with whom to talk, and not just the old got it here when they had it there cheaper sort of talk, but talk about why, and not just why this over why that, but why anything in the first place for this top-floor apartment, and why even the whole apartment. It was a complex issue, and no one would talk to her about the whys, therefore Fliegelman. She was glad to have Fliegelman here. Not glad to have just anyone to talk to, but Fliegelman specifically, because she knew that Fliegelman knew something and could help her with all of these whys, and not just the whys and why the whys, but get seriously down to the bottom of the whys and weigh things out. She was glad to have Fliegelman. She didn't know how she knew that he knew something, but he did, didn't he?

Yes, he did.

He saw, she told him. Yes, he saw. Mostly people didn't see and that was the problem for her. She had tried to talk to other people before about all of these whys, but they only told her to relax and do something, get a job, buy some clothes, take a class, talk to someone professionally although she wasn't crazy or anything, exercise, redecorate. Relax and do something. Talking about it, thinking on the whys, that was her problem, they told her, then they laughed and asked her was she going to tonight's soirée or didn't she think that this was quite something, this whatever they were wearing or holding or hanging.

She didn't want Fliegelman to get her wrong here. These were not stupid people, or even careless or thoughtless people. These people were the people who ran the city, in her circles, and they had all been everywhere and seen many things. In her circles they were rich and educated and beautiful. They were even kind and considerate, charitable. And they talked, but they detoured Mimi's questions, rerouting her to their things. Things and stuff, and only the whys and wherefores of things and stuff. Never the whys of why. How had she got to this place? Had she once known more about the whys and been derailed in her gathering life, or had only the whys creeped up on her lately?

She should explain. They, and she was saying we here, had always had every thing they had ever wanted; to ask for more would have been greedy, had they been able to think of more things to ask for. They had spent years perfecting every thing and finding every thing, and even though in the beginning of their quest Mimi had expected it to be a rude ascent, it had not been, every thing falling on to them like a hard rain. They had only had to stand out in it. It was so simple a quest then, they had to invent some hard myths to shirk their felicitous facility, and from there had to live out these myths, pretending that this easy life was hard. They stopped seeing each other quite so much, to live up to their falsified standards, and that, thought Mimi, was probably where things had started going wrong. It gave them time offstage in their drama. But that also was not the real problem, though it was very much like the real problem, but it was not what she was trying to get across to Fliegelman, who sat across from her. It was not just a question of they; it was a larger why.

Fliegelman had to remove his nagging question about the mysterious presence of Mimi's "we," read they. The reminder of it he had scribbled threatened to upset his second or third cup of coffee.

"Who's 'we,' Mimi?" he asked.

They were Mimi and her unexpected husband, Nion LeClair. They had been married for some time. They met when she was fresh out of college, working as a salesgirl in the tie department of a downtown store. He spent a lot of time hanging around, until one day he bought her a rose and she gave in to his many charges. He was handsome, a little older, tall and well-built, and he always wore the nicest, most expensive ties. He had been in business then, and he was in business now for himself. She had had a lot

of plans then for what the future might be, but she did not
see how marriage could interfere. That was too much of a
cliché. They lived for years outside of the city, but spent
most of their time here. Nion had told her that she was the
most beautiful woman he had ever met, and she helped him
help themselves to all the things that seemed to come so
easily. Now was different, of course, because that is the way
all these married women stories went, even those who married wealthy. He had invested so much of himself in the
business of creating his myth of difficult living that he was
always at the office, it seemed, or on the road. He was a
professional male. She grew bored and took up hobbies and
the rest, blah, blah, blah. Even their difficulties, the vast
separations that lived between them, were too easy, a for-
mula lifted from a thousand other stories. And they did
what most people did who were so disparate, and who were
not characters: they pretended to be happy and kept on the
lookout for more. Wasn't that just about the true case with
everybody? The horrible regularity of their easy problems
was the most terrifying pleasantry of them all. They were
happy now. Even that seemed too right, trite.

It wasn't them, or even Nion. It was something so far
deep down into all the whys she'd been laying on Fliegelman that she couldn't see through that murky water. Perhaps Fliegelman knew something new for her, something
totally outside the realm of her perfectly awful world. He
was not to get her wrong when she told him that she loved
her husband.

"Fliegelman," she said. "Talk to me."

Because she told him there was something heroically
wrong here in this city and this apartment, and she could

not put her finger on it. Because she had been looking and looking and never saw what she expected to see, and never saw anything unexpected.

"Listen to me, Fliegelman," she said. "Talk to me."

Had Fliegelman been listening harder he would have been behind her. Mimi had told him a great many things, but she was still not telling Fliegelman what he thought he would be hearing now, even though he had no idea what it was. She was dancing around what she was wanting to tell him, but the thing she wanted to say would be no partner, a shy wallflower of a statement that needed gentle coaxing.

Take the days, Fliegelman was telling her, take the days and hold them for a while in your hands. Look at them like playing cards and study their obverse faces. Look for the hidden marks on these taken days. Look carefully at what you see there in your hands, and I will tell you a story about the days, and maybe then something will dawn on us both.

He told her of his desire's dissolution, of the conspiracy of the days, of quitting business for retail, of gathering the little bits of his desire, of seeing Mimi over the city's face and trying to decipher her scattered desire. He told her all, and when he was done telling her, the old gray day was yawning and huffing and getting ready to hand over the controls to a night so much like the day, they might have the same name.

Mimi listened and made coffee. The apartment began to light itself, intensifying its illuminations as the day and night fumbled with the knobs of the city, and blue took over, an electric blue of clouds backlit, and the lights coming up all over the face of everything in orange and yellow sulfurous hues as beautiful as anything.

Fliegelman had to go. It was time to work. Mimi understood. He had stayed ahead of the day by invading its conspiracy, and it was time to work to stay ahead of the conspiracy. There would be more time now for each of them, however. They were on to something here.

Mimi came down that evening, while Fliegelman stood at the counter thinking of her above him. Mimi had come down the elevator to speak with Fliegelman about his conspiracy theory, if Fliegelman didn't mind. The conspiracy, it seemed, struck some major chords in her, and she was hoping they would fit in some minor discussions, if retail would permit. Sosii was shushed, the lull before the after-dinner rush and well before the before-movie crowd. Mimi had asked Fliegelman politely if they could talk, but her entrance to the store was too confident to be polite. She seemed to have the crowd situation scoped out. For Fliegelman this was one of retail's great gains: sometimes you got to lift your nose from the grindstone, and if it was slow, just be there, you just had to be there. It was more like being alive than working.

She had taken hold of Fliegelman's conspiracy, shook it hard and nothing fell out. He was right; the days had conspired to make the weekend bright and hopeful. She had engaged her calendar and found Fliegelman on the mark. She had felt the conspiracy herself and had been unable to sneak underneath it or around it or over it, it was so huge, and because it was so huge, it hid itself discreetly, right in front of your nose.

"Why are we different, Fliegelman?" she asked him. She was paging through a fashion magazine.

"I don't think we are," he said.

115

"Then how come we can see the conspiracy?"

"Just lucky," he said. "I guess, or unlucky."

"What can we do about it?"

"Who can stop the day?" he asked.

Mimi sat back on herself for a minute to think about it. The store fell away from her. Fliegelman thought she looked happy there, crouched by the cookbooks, thinking of the inevitability of the days and the days' successors. She was rocking. One strand of her hair, which had been pulled back, fell away and crossed her face.

"Fliegelman," she said, a whole sentence not intended to salute any forthcoming sentence; Fliegelman, period.

Then she continued.

"This is ridiculous. I should go. I'll talk to you later. It's starting to get busy."

"No," he said. "It is ridiculous, but stay, stay all night with me here. It's just getting good when it gets busy."

And busy it got, a sudden dizzy business, reminiscent of the weekend's fast fury. It could happen anytime, this swing from slow to fast, this frenzy.

First the grazers herded themselves in and spread out evenly, staking their territories of grazing. They were slowly working their way to desire, gathering little bits of it here and there, much like Fliegelman had been doing since he started at Sosii. The store hummed with their quiet watching.

The first to step forward and be counted were the disgruntled, those whose desire had turned on them at home, betrayed earlier moments of desire. They returned to Sosii to return in exchange for a new desire. They were first because their desire had been preying on them for days and often more than the two-week limit for returns. Mimi stood nearby, watching it all stock-still, thumbing through a book about midgets. Fliegelman's task was to stand at the counter and appease them.

The first of the first of the evening was a tiny old man in a checked coat and checked hat. He unraveled a large dictionary from a tattered, brown bag and set it on the counter in front of Fliegelman. He was triumphant.

"I want to return this dictionary, young man," the old man said. The old man barely peeked over the counter's top.

"What seems to be the problem?" asked Fliegelman, respecting retail's tone.

"I don't like it. It's not very good. I have thoroughly investigated its multitude of historically based definitions and find it lacking throughout. I find that I already know nearly one full half of the words in this povertized compendium. I am very disappointed with it on the whole, and must say, am very disappointed with this store, where, let me add, I spend hundreds of dollars every week. How could you carry such a dictionary as this? I am expecting nothing less than a full refund."

The little man thumped the counter with his thumb as he spoke.

"I see," said Fliegelman. "May I see your receipt, then?"

"No, you may not," said the little man, tugging on his lapels and straightening his hat.

"Have you lost it?" Fliegelman asked.

"No, of course not. I simply have no intention of showing it to you. The product is flawed and that is enough. You will please give me a refund immediately."

His voice was getting loud. The grazers were looking up.

Fliegelman stood his ground. He pointed to the sign on the front of the register that listed all the return provisions.

"Your name, young man," the old man said more than asked.

Fliegelman told him.

"I see, then. Quite right. Such a name. You are in great trouble now. I am personal friends with the owner of this shoddy establishment and will traffic no rudeness from you. You are a cretin and a thief, young man, and I will have your job for this."

The old man grabbed the dictionary from Fliegelman and stuffed it back into its crumple. Then he took off his hat ceremoniously and hit Fliegelman on the shoulder with it.

"It is obvious, you prostitute," said the old man, shaking and crimson, "that you do not know who I am, and you will suffer terribly for this, I promise you."

He shook the dictionary at Fliegelman.

"You will pay," he trembled, then turned and walked away. He minced quickly on his little old man legs to the pair of front doors. He tugged at one and found it locked, and so he tugged and tugged some more. With great dignity, he composed himself there, adjusted his hat, sidestepped once to the other door and left with great dispatch.

Everyone in the store looked away from everyone else, including Mimi from Fliegelman and he from her. Two clouds of opinion seemed to drift through the store, and Fliegelman felt the mist of them both; there were those who hated Fliegelman for what he had done, and those who admired him and pitied his position. Fliegelman changed the music to try and soothe all the parties.

Mimi moved into the back of the store. She was looking over books, over the tops of them at the other customers. Her green eyes hinted flecks of mica.

After a couple of small sales floated by Fliegelman— some thin sacks of blank greeting cards, sharp images of desire—a shy younger woman came to beg of Fliegelman a favor. Her favorite sister had given her this book—a bulky, green hardcover novel—and she was wondering if she might be able to exchange it because she, well, it was just a bit too much for her. She didn't have a receipt. Fliegelman assured her. She roamed to the fiction section and found three paperbacks that took the place of the one ugly brick, not as thick as the hardcover when piled up, but somehow multiplied. It was a fair exchange. She smiled at Fliegelman, with a soft entreaty that asked Fliegelman to please not tell her sister about it. When Fliegelman re-shelved the book, a card slipped out of it. He read it. Fondest wishes were sent over a thousand miles for a sister, and the book was a testimony to their enduring relationship. The novel her sister had sent was about submarine warfare and stamped with a book club's signature.

Mimi still scouted.

There was another exchange. A knapsacked young man in black came to the register with the paperback of a recent literary best-seller. Fliegelman could see, from the fluff of the pages, that a third of the book had already been read. The man, in owlish brown spectacles, wore muted blacks and grays. Fliegelman could see by his outfit that he was a public writer. His knapsack was of fine, worn leather, and sticking from it were bound, blank books. Finely tipped pens that matched his shirt peeked from his pockets. He wore his sensitivity like a glove. He was a journalist, copying his innermost thoughts while seated at cafés, where everyone could see him entertaining his personal muses. Fliegelman knew that part of the equipment for such an interior outing was an easily recognizable book, split open on the table, its cover showing.

The writer wanted to exchange a book that had been printed in shiny paperback editions of six differently colored covers. The writer wanted to exchange the book for the same book, but with another color cover. Fliegelman pulled the man's face out of his memory's hat. The writer had bought the book from Fliegelman last week. He had bought the one with the garish yellow cover, when last week he had been wearing a yellow wool pullover sweater and blue jeans. Fliegelman allowed the exchange. The writer chose the purplish cover from the six-layer stack near the counter. It matched.

Mimi wandered.

Then came a two heartbeat lull, the famous cartoon sucker-punch lull, just before the buying began. Fliegelman had felt it before and was ready for it. The tinkling of the cash register's bells alerted everyone. The buying and the questions came at once. They were off.

Soon everything was stacking upward and lining outward. Fliegelman's buzz shot out for help, and other clerks joined in to fight the tide of sudden desire. Bags got stuffed, charges phoned, phone numbers handed over. Impulse items flew in the fray. The line got longer. Fliegelman and company helped the customers who couldn't help themselves. It wasn't so much a purchase as a meal.

Did they have this in paperback, a woman wanted to know. Her sister had it in paperback in Texas, but she couldn't find it here. This book was on the radio and it had a blue cover, but they forgot what it was all about. They just had to find a new book on antique radios, it was urgent. Had they read any good books lately? What was that book on TV? What's the best thing they'd ever read they had to have? It was a necessity. Could they please have ten copies of that little red book because they gave it to all their friends as gifts all of the time, and it changed their lives. Was this any good, had they read this, was this getting good reviews? The questions like a blanket of arrows.

Fliegelman lost track of Mimi during the blitz because you lost track of everything during such an offensive. The only thing that remained loyal was the books themselves, the chunky, blocky, wonderfully thick, slick paper of it all. The books fit the hands well, as if they jumped into the hands, as if the thumb's opposable purpose. Their brute physical presence stayed tough.

Mimi succumbed to the giddifying night. She turned and whirled among the stacking shoppers, and the books flew into her hands.

"I want all these," she told him. He nodded and kept them with his.

She kept looking for the one that all the others had promised to be, and she just had to keep looking. She knew that the one she really wanted, the one that had her name written all over it, was still hidden in the alphabet. She felt its lurking. So she would keep looking for a little while yet. Fliegelman asked if he could help.

She didn't know precisely, but she would know it when she picked it up. It was a book, she imagined, that would read like a dream and tell her things she had known but had not been able to say. This one book would immerse her completely in its world and free her to see her own world; it would fill her up and leave her hungry.

On wore the night, furiously, aided and abetted by the store's openness. The customers totaled out and went back for more.

Sales billowed. Their stacks ascended and decreased. Each time they found a book, it was a good excuse to shelve one whose allure had already dimmed. The store, with its resources diminished, victorious, finally relented and closed. The shoppers were herded out, still asking for one last book. Fliegelman looked around and assessed the damage. It had been a good night.

"Ring me up, Fliegelman," said Mimi.

He ran the magic wand over the books' tags, and the code numbers, titles, and prices appeared on the green screen. With the push of a button, the numbers combined and expressed themselves on the bottom line of the terminal. Mimi feigned shock with delight when Fliegelman summarized her purchases for her. She put it on her MiracleVisa. Then Fliegelman ran the books over the metal box that demagnetized the strips of metal in the books. This was a security measure, he knew, but perhaps this device not only took the beep from the books, but stole their desirability from them and that was why everyone kept coming back for more. He filled two heavy bags with Mimi's achievements.

Fliegelman didn't have to pay. Retail let him borrow

what he wanted. Filling two heavy bags, he pretended that he owned the whole store.

He and Mimi straightened the store along with the other clerks. They pulled order and quiet over the messy store like a comforter over a rumpled bed, smoothing the folds and creases. Mimi and Fliegelman passed over all the books with great care, but left them there and refrained from taking more than they already had. The coffee bar mopped up, and the kids there had a smoke. It was time to close.

Fliegelman and Mimi were the last ones to leave. They stood outside the closed store's windows and looked back in to check on the work they'd done. The store was immaculate. The displays in the windows were still lit up and would stay that way all night. Fliegelman felt that they both felt that they wanted to go back into the store, that regrettably they had left something behind. The window's pane only added to their sense of loss, he felt. But finally they turned and walked away from the dormant store and the cold blue lights of the pastry cases in the Sosii café. Dragging their heavy bags, they walked slowly and talked through the empty, gurgling plaza to Mimi's inviting elevator.

Mimi's empty apartment waited eagerly for them. When she opened the front door, cradling her heavy load, the lights of the apartment came on of their own accord. It was as if no one lived there. The bitchin' pink surfboard glowed.

"Is Nion here?" Fliegelman asked. He fell back exhausted onto a chair that appeared to be made of yogurt cartons. His bags spilled slippery books on the cushy carpet.

"No," said Mimi. She had dropped her bags as she came into the room, unable to bear the burden any longer, and had gone off into the bedroom. She came back unchanged.

"No," she said. "He's away on business, as usual." She knocked herself down on the couch. "I swear, Fliegelman," she said. "Did you see us? That was awful. I can't believe we fell for the oldest trick. I'm ashamed. I thought we had royally seen through the whole desire scam. What the hell happened?"

"We saw through it, but that didn't stop it. I don't know, Mimi. Look at all this stuff."

He scattered all the books over the carpet. The books just sat there. Mimi sat up on the couch. Fliegelman wanted to look into Mimi's green eyes, but couldn't raise his own to hers to see that she was looking everywhere but at him.

"You know," Fliegelman said. "You can take them back. That's really no trouble. I'll take them back for you, if you'd like."

"It's not that," she said. "It's not that at all. They're nice books, really. We both know that. I'll read them sometime, I'm sure. As soon as they don't embarrass me any longer. In the store I was sure it was the books, but now I see the books have nothing to do with it. I still want, Fliegelman, and I still don't know the whys."

Fliegelman stared.

"Do you know what comes next, Fliegelman? Standing here on all this used up desire. Do you know what we are supposed to do? Do we just stand here? Do you know what we do now? How are we supposed to live? We know too much, and we know too little. What do we do with it all?"

Fliegelman knew nothing. It had been so long since he had felt his desire full upon him; the scattered bits had coalesced finally. He had lost his desire, he had thought it was for good, and thought it for the best. Then he had been betrayed by a conspiracy wrought with desire, and he had sneaked beneath its barbed wires. He had gathered up his desire again in manageable little bits, he'd thought, and somehow gained a hold on it. But now his desire had reared up again and taken him away from what he thought he knew. Desire had bowled him over, and he'd struck out. He knew nothing to throw back at Mimi's questions. He was sorry. His desire had embodied itself again, and it sat across from him. To speak was to loose it. Old man gray night was laughing at him.

Their desire was getting out of hand, according to Mimi.

"I'm going to change again," she said. "Stay here and make yourself comfortable. It will only take a minute."

Fliegelman wandered the vast living room. The minute lasted forty at least. The apartment which earlier had dazzled him with its lushness, was now a desert of barren things that had been demagnetized like the books. He wanted to leave, but he was devoid of such strength. He gathered the fallen books into neat pyramids, but that new shape regenerated nothing. He looked out on the city, but the gray night had swallowed this tall apartment, and he saw nothing but the gauzy fabric of night's cloak.

Mimi returned. She was a spectacle to behold. She wore a column of shivering lights, blue and silver, evening's gown of far too rich apparel. Her perfect hair was done up

125

and pulled back. Glittering jewels pierced her ear and braided around her neck. The dress constricted her in walking so that she came on to him in small glides. Her shoes were black leather sophisticates, and they supported her airiness. Black stockings showed off her fine calves. The dress parted with itself below her knee on one side and snaked a leggy path to her thigh. The rest of her body fell into place. Fliegelman stopped himself right there and just stared.

"It is nice, isn't it?" she asked. "But now you. Go in there and put on what I've laid out for you. Then I have a surprise."

Fliegelman did as he was told. In the bedroom on the enormous bed he found a blue silk, Italianate suit as perfect as Mimi's dress.

"Don't worry," she called. "One size fits all."

He shed himself and donned the new suit. It hung perfectly, of course, and the shiny textures brought new meanings to the word fit.

When he came back in, Mimi held lightly two champagne tulips. The room's color had come back. Somehow, following the cue of what they were wearing, the room had blued up. She had pulled back panels, setting off the television's large screen. She asked Fliegelman to sit on the appropriate couch. She had something she wanted to show him.

"You've never seen anything like this before," she said. "I guarantee it. You won't see anything like this anywhere else. Strictly a one of a kind deal here."

Mimi pulled a black, unmarked, book-shaped box from the shelves, clicked it open and freed a video cassette. She pushed the cassette into the top of the television, which swallowed it. The screen buzzed blue.

"Are you ready?" she asked. She picked up the remote tuner and sat on the arm of the now blue couch where Fliegelman sat holding his champagne by the stem.

"Cheers," she said, and they clanked their crystals. She aimed the tuner at the screen and triggered the tape rolling.

The screen went black and silent. Mimi put her hand on Fliegelman's shoulder. The sound of a broken-glass wind chime filled the room, then faded. White words spelling out FOR PRIVATE USE ONLY came up briefly then dissolved. The black enlightened and gave way to blue; soft music walked quietly around them. The screen showed off a blue room where a couple stood at gauzy curtains and gazed out on a rainy blue street in what looked like a European capital. The camera breezed through the room's antiques and wound up behind the couple, showing them full length. The man had his arm around the woman. She tilted her head to his shoulder, and they both held champagne tulips. There was a sudden sharp cut to a sepia picture of moving brown sheets and bedclothes; the cut lasted two seconds. The music stayed constant. The camera moved closer to the couple, then there was another cut to the same sepia scene, an imperceptibly shorter cut, and still the music stayed constant. The camera moved closer to the couple at the window, then cut again to sepia, then back to the couple, then to sepia, switching back and forth between the window scene and the moving bed sheets, and all the time getting closer to the couple at the window, and all the time shortening the length of the cuts, until finally the camera stopped in the blue room and stayed focused on the heads of the two lovers. The two heads turned slowly to look at one another, revealing their profiles. It was Mimi and Fliegelman.

Fliegelman twitched involuntarily at the recognition. Mimi looked down at him, smiling, her bright green eyes shaded by the room's mood.

Fliegelman turned back to the screen and saw himself and Mimi still there, gazing into one another's eyes. He tried to swallow hard. The camera stayed focused on them, then began to move up and over them, and flew out the window into the rainy sky of the old world city, shining bright blue, then fading again to black.

"I don't understand," said Fliegelman, staring at the television as the black gave way again to another apartment scene, but this one in real colors.

"Isn't it wild?" she asked. "Keep watching while I explain. It gets even better. There are five hidden video cameras pointed at us right now: one in front, one in back, one on each side, and one looking down on us. They feed our images into a special computer that transmits them to this already made videotape. The cameras can pick out our heads because of a special heat-sensitive lens. Notice that's our hair there."

She was right. On the screen Mimi and Fliegelman sat down to an extravagant dinner, and there was Mimi's perfect hair, caught in all its glorious colors. They were eating lobsters.

"The computer," she whispered as Fliegelman watched, "has a special program that uses our basic facial features to extrapolate our entire realm of expressions. Watch how right it gets the way we eat."

It was flawless. Nowhere on the screen was there any evidence of a computer's intrusion. It was the real thing; it was Mimi and Fliegelman there where they had never been together, doing something that they had never done together. It was shocking. It was like unearthing a memory that had been packed away for sixteen years, and like such memories, it carried wariness along with it. Danger seemed imminent to Fliegelman.

"Incredible, but true," whispered Mimi, still whispering. Her hand was on Fliegelman's neck tightly.

The video story continued. The couple ate their dinner and chatted, though there was no sound other than the music, but as the dinner went on with its rich foods, caviars and mousses and oysters and pâtés, the music faded, as did the picture. When the picture came back up, the soundtrack insinuated a beat, driving and forceful, which came up strong and soon was joined by a jazzy, synthesized, wordless tune. The tune commandeered the images, and soon the film was off on a whirlwind of colliding collage, cutting back and forth in obedient time. It showed the couple in various places, in various poses, laughing, crying, embracing, dancing on a broad avenue in the middle of the morning's first wake. Their clothes were constantly changing, but their faces stayed the same. The images became more sexually charged, and Fliegelman faced himself on a black couch in a black room where Mimi lay in a black skimpy dress that almost revealed her perfect breasts, and he was touching her with a piece of jagged ice, touching her under the chin and then pulling the ice down her neck to the cleavage of her perfect breasts. When he stopped there, she grabbed his hand and moved it back to under her chin, and he retraced the trail of water he had left on her perfect, excited skin. This scene was broken up by scenes of him and Mimi standing on a street corner in the rain. Fliegelman held an umbrella, and Mimi wore a fur. They were laughing and talking, and suddenly Mimi pulled a piglet from under her fur and danced it along through the air backward and forward. There were many little scenarios like this, but they were hard to pick out because they were all superimposed on one another and reversed and turned upside down and shot in different lights. There was no story to the video, just shot upon shot of Mimi and Fliegelman or whoever this faceless couple was wearing their faces, and them dancing and singing and talking and lying in bed and stroking one another and almost having their clothes fall off and long, luscious kisses that lasted probably minutes if the breaks weren't there. The pace quickened as the video continued. The story was replaced by rhythm.

"What's it called?" Fliegelman asked.

"It's too new for a name yet," she said. "They're working on that right now. Nion brought it home for me. He's invested heavily in it."

The hour-long video built to a fever pitch and ended with Mimi and Fliegelman staring out the same window that had opened the video. The fading cuts of the sepia-toned bedclothes now were still.

They were stunned. Mimi still sat on the arm of the couch, her arm round Fliegelman's neck. Fliegelman stared at the black screen that soon went fuzzy under his still staring. He didn't know what to say.

Mimi rose and extracted the cassette from the television. She put the tape in its case, stroked the cool vinyl cover, and put the case in its place. She shut off the television. She grabbed Fliegelman's hand and pulled him up out of the couch. She led him to the bedroom, where she stopped him on the near side of the bed. With a clap of her hands the bedroom lights dimmed. She went to the far side of the bed, and without saying a word, began to undress for Fliegelman.

With her long, red-nailed, thin, perfect hands, she caressed her own body over the blue, shivering dress, running her hands over her breasts down to her thighs. She reached behind her and unzipped her dress down to her waist. The dress loosened in front. She pulled the dress off her shoulders by its thin straps and down and away from her, letting it fall to the floor.

Fliegelman would be lying if he were to say he hadn't thought of seeing Mimi naked.

She stepped delicately out of the dress's huddled mass, but she was not naked. A black slip and her black stockings and shoes masked her body. She turned around slowly once. She was in a perfect shape.

She looked down at her cleavage, and Fliegelman followed. He thought that these breasts he could almost see now were the breasts he almost saw in the video. Mimi drew her fingernails lightly over the exposed skin of her breast. She grabbed and gathered the silk slip near her waist and revealed a lacy black garter belt and panties. She pulled the slip over her head, tossed it across the room. She wore a black lacy bra through which he could almost see the white skin of her breasts and her dark nipples. She was wearing her shoes and had not yet become naked. He looked hard at the tops of her thighs where they were exposed between the stockings and her panties, and at the flat curve of her stomach and the fine hair that drew a peaked line there. All of her skin that he could clearly see was tanned bright brown and smooth.

Kneeling on the bed, her thigh muscles tensing and her buttocks pushed back and up, she gestured to Fliegelman to take off his coat, and he did, but when he started to unbutton his shirt, she shook her head, and he stopped. She beckoned him with a long finger. He slipped out of the pointy, borrowed Italian shoes and climbed onto the bed, kneeling, face to face with Mimi. She put her arms around him and kissed him, and when she pulled away to look at him, he saw her beautiful face close up, the perfect lines and curves of her almost too beautiful face, the serene face, the angry face, the laughing, taunting, inquisitive face, the young and old face, the face that stared back wonderingly under her perfect, hard to define hair. He stared into her jade-green eyes and could not pull away from them, trapped by them, falling deeper and deeper into them.

Mimi leaned back, clapped again, and the lights went out. She leaned forward into Fliegelman, clasping him tightly. They fell over onto the bed. Mimi undressed him in the dark, and he undressed her completely. He kissed her behind the ear and tasted her base makeup.

They tangled. They groaned. They lip-locked. They fell over heads and heels. They traced the soft maps of each other's bodies. They sought out hillocks and flats and climbed and grazed and rested and started.

In the naked dark, Fliegelman found Mimi completely alone with him. He no longer tasted her makeup when she gave up her neck to him. The cold night outside flew round and round the Holiday Plaza and tried desperately to get to them and mock them both in their bed in the dark room which was the same dark room everyone slept in, but they were safe from the night here and the night's cruel vision. Holding on to one another, they fell asleep in the bedroom that was strewn with their mess.

THE TWO-SIDED CITY

□

This was the city of joy. Fliegelman knew it right off. Lying in the crumpled bed in the early hours of the new day's first rounds, he heard the wet tires swishing on the streets below and knew that the city had taken itself by storm, and that the old gray season, which had at first been his blanket, then his betrayal with its sharp weekends, had given way to the next season. The conspiracy had fallen; he could hear it all the way up in the tower. The rains had torn away the fog's muffling sweater, bringing back the city's timbres and tones which were music to his ears. The knife swish was the cars' sideling shuttle on the slippery streets. He heard above that the intermittent, lower whoosh of the streetcars' passings and the thundering rumble of the big trucks. Voices pinged off the sides of buildings and echoed up to him, sharp, senseless. He heard the whole city wakening to the new season and felt he could almost hear the sloshing of feet, the snapping of umbrellas, sighs, whispers, the zipping of coats, the frantic searches for coins in the bottoms of lumpy bags, purses clicking open, the clank of the quarter in the bottom of a streetcar's bucket, the sucking noises of the gutter filtered through the last season's dead leaves, and the calming hiss of the streetcar's auto-matic doors enclosing the wet riders in their warm coaches.

Mimi slept, still, and Fliegelman took pains not to wake her. He listened for a good hour to the city's unexpected song. He did not want to break anything just yet, but wanted to let it go on, this singing, zinging song.

Mimi stirred eventually, enough to let Fliegelman res-cue himself from her obscene heaviness. He dressed and hushed to the kitchen. Standing at the windows there, the city exceeded itself, a silver baron city, gleaming under the high, dark clouds. As he watched the fish-silvery city, the colors galvanized themselves, the aggressive colors of the city in rain. The red neon hotel sign, four stories tall three blocks away, was no ordinary red sign in neon, but a laser ruby sign that could probably be seen from space. The green and yellow soft drink sign on the corner across from the hotel was more than lemon and lime advertising itself, it was lemon and lime juice concentrated syrup, and enough concentrated to fill several lakes when diluted. Even the blacks and whites of a lost little police car were no ordinary absences of spectral color. The black was the painterly thick oil black of all colors painted on top of one another and another and another until the black came first but all colors hid there and made themselves known in glimpses; and the white was not just pure light, but the whitest light of the canvas sucked clean by a terrible vacuum, leaving nothing but white and the trails of the fleeing colors. The colors of this city were competing for space in an all-out assault.

He ground out some coffee. The clean apartment sucked up the roasting aromas, the brown, hot, welcoming odors that ordered some hot buns and butter to go with the coffee. The well-mannered kitchen pointed everything out to Fliegelman, and the agreeable table set a cozy place for both of them.

The bags of the new books looked fresher now than they had after last night's hectic shopping. He picked up an essay on streetcars, and breathing in the beautiful coffee, began to read. He fell for the crisp print and thumbed the rough edges. He read lightly, leaving the city room enough to perch on his shoulder and look on with him. He did not want the city to go away.

Mimi tumbled in, wearing a fresh, clean bathrobe. They said nothing to one another, but signaled their silences to correspond. Mimi stood at the open window. Her lime-green eyes stole glances of everything.

They spent their breakfast together quietly, reading and eating; the day befriended them.

The city cleansed itself all through the early hours, while Mimi and Fliegelman showered and bathed and took possession of what they had nearly lost the night before. Afternoon inserted itself into the day's original plan with a show of broken clouds, the light breaking golden on the city's surfaces like a thousand floating coins. Unlike the previous season's demanding, clear weekend days, this day's afternoon cooled itself and threw shadows for hiding; it had come to highlight the city, not overthrow its governors. The day, the morning rain and the afternoon's rain of scattered light, had come with a new attitude. The air was spiked with the scent of change, a sensation that claimed that the new season had gathered the rotting growth of the previous season and mingled this stench with rain's stark power, fomenting a sweet, sour smell of death reborn. The claim was not morose, but cheerful. The season talked of change and pointed out the specific examples, hiding nothing, revealing all, and pointed, not behind, but ahead. The scents of the turning wheel.

Mimi and Fliegelman left the apartment behind, fell to steaming earth and went out into the day, not bowing to a superior command, but willfully. The day was an open book, not required reading. They seemed to float and fly over the city, touching down now and then for a quick score, running after points of interest. They levitated, following winds and hobnobbing with everything and everyone in sight, and they kept up their peregrinations for a day and then another day and then continuing on. The days glued themselves together into a huge kite of days that dipped and leveled according to the spidery strings of his Mimi and her Fliegelman. Fliegelman kept working, and Mimi came to see him there, sharing discreetly timed dinner breaks. Otherwise, they built the city to their own liking, day after seamless day.

Even the weekends, contrary to Fliegelman's fear, had calmed down, mixing equal parts of light and shade, and always finding themselves chilled by evening's arrival, the warm scents of the day shift carrying through the calming evenings' starts. The city was back in good hands.

Fliegelman shelved all his questions of Nion, and Mimi didn't seem ready for the cross-exam anyway. Nion never walked in on their conversations, didn't saunter around their room hoping to be noticed with shock like a dead war hero revived. He was missing in this action. No photos represented him skillfully in his defense. He was a man lost in the time that land forgot. He was barely a ghost, perhaps just the light flicker of a curtain moved by the breeze of a ghost passing in the next room. Mimi and Fliegelman made a good case of his absence. The days went on without him.

The only chink in Fliegelman's joyous armor was his uneasiness over Mimi's call on his apartment. She had wanted to see it immediately, but he had stalled her at her apartment. He wanted her to see where he lived, wanted to have her there, to show her his life and his church, but was uneasy at the prospect of her seeing his meager four rooms. She came from a different world. What if his small accommodations should push her away?

Since the new season, Fliegelman himself had visited his apartment occasionally, exchanging his laundry, but on those occasions he had been taken by his apartment's comforts, the soft beds and couches and chairs and views. The new season had opened his eyes, and he saw again his church out one side and the ocean slope out the other. It was not a prison, but a way station, warm and dry.

His uneasiness was easily drowned by the torrent of everything else, a tiny pebble washed away, smoothed and obliterated. Fliegelman finally asked Mimi to join him there. They were set.

He would take her the long way, giving both of them time to reconsider and distract themselves. They'd walk.

He picked her up and they walked out of the humming Holiday Plaza, past the shops and Sosii, too, and found themselves under a scattered herd of cloud cows in an otherwise speckless sky. The city opened twelve ways before them. Fliegelman went right, Mimi following. At the corner streetcar stop three people waited while Sam's luncheoneers watched. A cool breeze ruffled everything. Birds wheeled. The red and white streetcar screeched up, but Fliegelman and Mimi let it go by with a second thought, the driver giving them a suspicious eye. It pulled away from them, and they followed it slowly, it making tracks, diminishing. The Plaza shadowed them, so they crossed the street to higher ground. They loped along toward Fliegelman's apartment far away on the other side of the city.

They walked with their arms around one another for a while, and even when they weren't, they still had their arms around one another, all tied up in those knots they were bound to feel.

They passed along empty streets of quiet apartments and quieter houses. Windows opened and shook out rugs, the dust catching the day and fluffing the suddenly alchemical motes. A pair of feet looked on the street's view from one apartment's window, the same window sharing loud music. A flung pencil leaped from the window to an untimely demise. The broad sidewalks gave Mimi and Fliegelman ample space for the weaving they undertook. The hills went up, and catching their breaths at the top over the view, Mimi and Fliegelman followed them down into pleasant little valleys of more of the same.

Finally they crested the hill that began Fliegelman's neighborhood, the ocean shimmering but invisible. He pointed toward the great ocean bridge for Mimi. Descending into the flats, they passed the tiny market where Fliegelman bought his little parcels of food and supplies three or four times a week. The grouchy shopkeeper who ran the larder stood at the window, and though he had never seemed to notice Fliegelman, he now waved and smiled through his clenched cigarette and the hanging ducks. Smiling also, Fliegelman waved back and pointed at the day.

When they got to his apartment, he fumbled purposefully with his keys to give the apartment a few seconds warning. His mailbox, usually empty save assorted presorted junk mail, was overflowing today with white, stamped bounty. There was no elevator here with climate control and looking-glass eyes, only three sharp turns of slanting stairs. Fliegelman babbled the whole way, distracting Mimi from the dust and mouse holes. He opened his apartment, swinging the door wide open.

Mimi was her glowing self as she walked through the four small rooms, leaving Fliegelman stranded with his wariness. He opened windows to relieve the hot pressure. Breezes raced around for moments, then calmed down and got to work. Mimi's apartment had no breezes except the forced air of her building's basement engines. To open a window on her twenty-third floor was to welcome high-level disturbances. Fliegelman's low-flying apartment was just right for a gentle swirl.

Fliegelman pieced together the obligatory coffee, while Mimi made her rounds, calling out her first lasting impressions. She urged Fliegelman to look at everything she looked at, though he couldn't see from the kitchen what she saw, and even though he had seen it a thousand times before.

"Look at these books, look at these records, this couch, this chair, this wonderful old table. Look at the bathroom, I mean really look at this. It's perfect. Look at the bedroom, look at those windows, look at that view. I bet you get to see a lot of sunsets from here. Look at that desk. Look at the size of those closets," looked Mimi, and Fliegelman saw, through her looking, his apartment for the first time again, and he forgave his apartment for all the other apartments it had never been.

"Look at this apartment," she said. "Look at the size of it. Look at the charm, the charm is just oozing off it."

It was perfect, she told Fliegelman as they sat down with their coffees on the old torn couch. She sat with her legs beneath her, sipping her coffee, and staring around the room with her greedy, green eyes.

"Look at these cups," she told Fliegelman. "They're great." And they were.

Fliegelman got up and went to the one window that still said nothing. He had been saving this, what he thought of as the apartment's best feature. With a grand tah-dah he pulled up the blind and presented in full living color his church.

The church was no longer hidden by the orange, slanting walls of fog, nor blighted by the day's blanched lights of last season. It sat there in all its glory for Mimi and Fliegelman to see, caressed by the changing season's softer tones, the hues of the huge marbles touched by greens and oranges and blues and purples, all lightly touched by them, washed watercolors by them.

He couldn't think of a thing to say. Mimi told him not to say a word. She believed in his church.

They sat in Fliegelman's apartment for hours watching the church, Mimi convincing Fliegelman that she loved his apartment and felt perfect and at home there. As the day climbed slowly down its own far side, the church turned the wheel of colors on itself, never the same church twice, never different. The calm gave way to talking, as the day

slowly shifted to evening and its light darkness and its serene face.

"We never finished, Fliegelman," said Mimi. "We only
got so far when we got caught up in something big. Remember? What are we going to do with all this desire?"

"I guess we'll just have to learn to live with it," he said.
"There doesn't seem to be much else to do, does there? We
both tried to get rid of it, get over it, tried to get it back
when we lost it, tried to get it to work for us, tried to get
it to obey, but it always gets back to the two of us, no matter
how we get it figured. When we get ornery with it, it gets
out of hand. We just have to let it get under our skins and
get to the heart of things, no matter what. Where does it
get us to try and get away? We can't get off. We better get
used to it."

"I get it," she said and smiled up at him. Having settled
into Fliegelman's apartment, and they were getting serious
about their comfort.

The phone had other plans for them. Oddly, it was for
Mimi.

"Hi," she said imperatively, knowing in advance who
was there on the other end. "With some friends. Great. I'll
see you there."

She laid the phone carefully in its cradle. She had to go.
She turned away from the church. Nion was back. He knew
she was here because she had dialed some numbers into a
machine that forwarded all calls, a deal she had made with
her husband. She had to go, and she would talk to Fliegelman soon. She was sorry, she told him, and she looked
sorry, too. The apartment was surprisingly empty.

Fine days went by, but Fliegelman spent them looking at other things, smaller things, and he hardly noticed them. Mimi was not phoning. She was not anywhere.

At Sosii Fliegelman kept his eye on the door, hoping she'd walk through it unhurt. The books at Sosii stared back at him. He staked out the coffee bar, but Mimi took no meals there. He cordoned off the Plaza at his breaks, questioning the passersby, but their vacant looks offered no clues. He walked the city and hoped for the random connection, some sight of Mimi entrenched in her desire's coat again, but all he saw were faces without her green eyes. The days were no friends of his, though they kept trying to contact him.

Nine days later the phone rang. Fliegelman knew it wasn't Mimi by the ring. Yet he picked up the phone because what could you say to the unanswered phone. After all, it was a simple piece of plastic with a wiry heart. He held the push-button phone with his fingertips at a long distance from his face, as if the mouthpiece might bite him or the earpiece hear his discombobulation and spread it all around town. He was hiding.

He waited for the phone to go first. Mumbling greeted him, then he heard the sound of a man, hoarse and low.

"Mr. Fliegelman," the man said pleasantly, "Are you there?"

Fliegelman tried to put the phone down, but it persuaded him to hang on a little bit longer.

"Mr. Fliegelman," the man said, more pleasantly than before. "This is Nion LeClair, Mimi's husband." His voice went up in tone, finishing the answered question.

"Yes, I see," said Fliegelman.

"Mr. Fliegelman," the man said, even more pleasantly.

"I know you're probably concerned about Mimi, as close as I understand you two have become recently, and I just want you to know that she is fine and sends her best wishes to you. She's out right now. Which is partly why I'm phoning right now. You see, Mr. Fliegelman, I'm phoning because I think you and I have some few things to talk about, regarding Mimi, and I was hoping to see you in person sometime soon to settle this unquiet matter, if it's not too inconvenient for you. I understand you are a very busy man, and I would hate to put you out."

"Yes, I see," said Fliegelman, the phone having got the smart part of his tongue.

"Well, Mr. Fliegelman," said Nion. "If we could get together sometime soon, that would be appreciated, if you follow me there. Do you follow me, Mr. Fliegelman? Just a chat. But don't answer just yet, because, Mr. Fliegelman, I want to personally assure you that there's really no harm anywhere, and this is solely intended as a matter of getting to know one another, Mr. Fliegelman. Getting the lay of the land, so to speak, Mr. Fliegelman. Mr. Fliegelman?"

"Why, yes, I guess that would be okay," said Fliegelman, beginning to stir, but unable to think of anything pleasant to say. "When should we—"

"Now, Mr. Fliegelman, what would you say to today, say, in a few minutes?" Nion put forth state of the art pleasantness. "I can have you picked up by my car in, say, ten or fifteen minutes, if that suits you, Mr. Fliegelman. And do please tell me if it is inconvenient for you right now, Mr. Fliegelman."

Fliegelman did not want in any way to meet Mimi's husband, a man he had tried with great equanimity to avoid, but he found the pleasantness of Nion's voice persuasive. He agreed.

"Well, that's just fine, Mr. Fliegelman," Nion said with what Fliegelman guessed to be the last of his life's supply of pleasantness. "I do have your address. My driver will leave immediately. I thank you very much, Mr. Fliegelman, and look forward to our meeting. Goodbye now."

The phone was dead, and Fliegelman did his part to kill it on his end. Fliegelman plopped and waited. Thoughts tried to run through his head, but were crushed by huge cement blocks of nothingness. All he could manage to get through the traffic congesting in his brain was, Materialize, Mimi. Make yourself known.

The endless wait was soon over. Answering to a honk that was more like a carillon, Fliegelman made the long walk down his short hall and his dangerous stairs, where a long, white car waited for him with open doors. The windows of the car were blackened, and he saw no sign of a driver. When he got into the dark interior, the driver was hidden again by a sheet of smoked glass between his seat and Fliegelman's passenger seat. The inside of the car was as big as Fliegelman's living room. He had expected to see a wet bar and a television, other accouterments of rented luxury, but no. There was only a spartan phone in the thick crush of the leathery odor.

The flawless ride was uninterrupted by any jammed traffic. Even the lights turned green when they spotted the big, white car. Fliegelman hoped there would be music, at least some Muzak to make him hum and jingle, but no sounds came at all, not even the sounds of the city outside. The short drive took an eternity, and in that time Fliegelman developed some superb answers to supposedly dumb questions, raised hundreds of defenses for thousands of offensive accusations, knowing full well his tongue would give up on him when the time came. The time came.

The big door creaked soundlessly open when the car stopped in front of Holiday Plaza. Fliegelman got out fast, but didn't catch the driver who sped sharklike away, disappearing underground. The Plaza was empty, even Sosii looked closed. The security man in the lobby waited in the wings for him.

"Mr. Fliegelman," he said from the open elevator. "Right this way, please. Mr. LeClair is waiting for you."

Downcast, Fliegelman hopped on. The security presence boarded with him. The big blue suit didn't push one of the tiny buttons, however. Instead, he opened a hidden door in the elevator's control panel, revealing a button marked simply with a T. He pushed that button, and the elevator began its controlled ascent, passing all the floors, even Mimi's twenty-three.

"Here we are at the top," said Fliegelman's gross companion. "Where the air is fresh and clear."

The security guard sang the last phrase in a lounge lizard's bell-clear tone. Fliegelman stepped out of the elevator, his ears popping, and the door closed behind him, becoming a large framed painting on a wall. There was no lobby here. It was one large office, so large it was many large offices, the largest office he had ever seen.

The walls of the penthouse were glass. The elevator's fake painting and shaft were the only walls here. At the far end of the room, which was round in contrast to the tower's square, was an enormous desk with an empty chair seated behind it. On the desk, Fliegelman saw coming closer, there was nothing but a phone, a note pad, and a silver pen.

Everything was black including the desk, phone, chair, and carpet. Only the note pad, the pen, and the windows weren't black. Even the light seemed black.

Fliegelman looked out past the desk to the city spread below him.

The fake painting divided its image with a whoosh, and Fliegelman turned to see a man in the most expensive of Italian suits Fliegelman had ever seen, even in the shop windows of downtown's smallest stores. Fliegelman could tell this from his mile away by the suit's sharp edges, as if wearing it would be a hazardous duty. The suit spoke to him.

"Mr. Fliegelman, I presume," it said pleasantly. "How nice of you to come. I'm Nion LeClair."

The suit came forward, and eventually, as it bore down on him, a face emerged.

What else could Fliegelman have expected? The face was perfect, as was the hair, as was the body that held it all together, though that may have been the suit's tailoring. He made out nothing of the man's features, nothing of his characteristics, nothing save the aura of perfections that made him up. Nion glowed with perfection.

He shook Fliegelman's hand heartily, and Fliegelman mumbled about pleasures, no problems. He turned Fliegelman around with his handshake, and still holding his hand in the manly fashion, put his other hand behind Fliegelman's back and guided him toward the picturesque windows.

"It's certainly a pleasure, it's certainly a thrill," Nion

said, telegraphing his professional radio pleasantries and finally letting Fliegelman's right hand at ease.

He walked Fliegelman to the window and stood there with him, his left hand barely touching his back though making itself known. He stared out the window, saying nothing, gazing magnificently down on the city, and Fliegelman followed suit. Then Nion sighed and spoke.

"Marvelous, isn't it?" he asked rhetorically. "Enough, however. Let's talk, shall we, Mr. Fliegelman?"

He freed Fliegelman's back, but with the same hand offered Fliegelman the whole office with a palming gesture. Fliegelman walked ahead slowly, not knowing which portion of the vast office was his to fill. Nion walked to the desk and stood behind the big chair.

"I'd offer you a seat, Mr. Fliegelman," he said, contritely pleasant now. "But as you see, there is only one chair, and I have a back problem. Do you mind, Mr. Fliegelman?"

"Not at all," said Fliegelman, wandering in a specific rectangle in front of the desk. "Please, sit down. I'm used to standing. In my job."

"Thank you, thank you, Mr. Fliegelman," he said. "Yes, your job. Downstairs, correct?"

Fliegelman nodded, and Nion sat, the chair expiring with comfort. Nion fidgeted with the note pad and pen, arranging them severely. Fliegelman looked at the elevator painting, his back to the desk.

"Now then, Fliegelman," Nion said, surprising the addressee, who turned and suddenly found himself no longer a mister.

"May I call you Fliegelman?" he said, leaning over the big desk. "And you do call me Nion," he said to Fliegelman, who had not called him anything.

"Now then, Fliegelman," he said pleasantly. "Where do we begin?"

Fliegelman stood in front of the desk with his hands crossed, a bad schoolboy.

"Fliegelman," he said, querulously kind, shaking his head slowly. "You have, I hate to say it, but you have, well, you have upset, shall we say, things. Yes, you've upset things, Fliegelman, and it's quite disturbing to us. Yes, quite."

Nion appeared to be reading the side of the silver pen.

"What are we going to do, Fliegelman?" he said, swiveling in his narrow chair. "What are we going to do?"

He swiveled back on Fliegelman; Fliegelman stayed put.

"First, the facts. We know what you've been doing with our Mimi, don't we Fliegelman, and I don't see how we can allow that to go on, can we? It is wrong, and we were wrong to let it happen in the first place, weren't we, Fliegelman?"

Fliegelman looked all ways about the room, trying to pin down the elusive, traitorous pronoun "we" that seemed incapable of forging alliances.

"Yes, you've upset things, Fliegelman," he said leaning again toward Fliegelman, as if Fliegelman were talking and Nion deaf to all tongues. "And mostly they are our things, and we will not allow that."

The pleasantness was gone. In its place there was something that Fliegelman couldn't name but could only shiver to. Fliegelman saw no crack in Nion's obvious perfection, but felt instead a gloomy ghost henchman standing behind the big desk.

"Please answer me, Fliegelman. What are we going to do?"

Fliegelman had no time for answers now, the questions backing up badly and stumbling over one another.

"How did you find out?" asked Fliegelman feebly. He thought he had asked the question with a forceful voice, but the air betrayed him.

"Cameras, my good friend," said Nion, leaning back a tilt. "There are cameras everywhere these days. Example. The cameras that filmed you and Mimi. Did you think they were blind? Did you think we didn't see? Did you think they were alone, those wonderful cameras? No, my friend. Cameras are never alone, and they don't miss a trick. It's all on film. There's no denying it."

Fliegelman saw.

"And what exactly will we do about it, Fliegelman?" he asked, getting up from behind the desk and walking to the window, his hands crossed behind his back. "We'll tell you, since you seem to have no answers. We never expected you to have answers, by the way. We've thought long and hard on this, Fliegelman. We've come to a decision, and it is one you cannot escape. We have thought of everything. There is no way out."

What Fliegelman had sensed before surrounded him now. He knew these things. It was imminent and violent; it was threat.

"But first," Nion said, his back still to Fliegelman. "We will tell you what we are not going to do to you. Because we thought long and hard on that as well."

Nion began to walk around the round room, his arms folded. He followed the curvature of the room, sticking close to the windows.

"We are not going to kill you," he said smugly. "We are not going to tear you limb from limb, or burn your eyes with a hot poker. We will not torture you in some dark cell and make you blaspheme your own mother. We are not going to squeeze your testicles in a vise grip, my good friend. We will not break your legs and throw you in the river. We will not hound you and drive you mad. We will not beat you to a bloody pulp personally, with our own two hands."

Nion kept up his walk.

"No, my friend," he said, threat following him like a film director's yes-men. "No, Fliegelman. We are not going to stoop to any of that. And do you know why?"

Fliegelman did not.

"Because," Nion said, holding up one finger, but not arresting his progress. "Because we have learned a lot, we have. That may be fine for other countries, may be a workable concept for them, but not for us. Not for us. We have refined ourselves, Fliegelman. It shows, doesn't it? We have learned that that sort of thing only leads us to trouble. No, Fliegelman, we have gone way beyond that barbarity. We are civilized men.

"But don't get us wrong," he said from the far side of the office, stopped now and looking at Fliegelman. "It's not that that wasn't our first instinct. It was. We wanted to kill you. You had upset things, and we were upset with you. We wanted to be ghastly. But we weren't. And why not? Because we've learned, and we know that killing you is nothing. We have better ways. We are civilized men, after all. We are not going to kill you, Fliegelman. We will ruin you. Ruin is what we are after."

Nion stopped and walked quickly across the office, straight for Fliegelman. Fliegelman stood stock-still, waiting for the blow, but Nion zoomed past him to the desk again.

"But we digress," he said, looking up with a smile. "You want Mimi, do you? Well, you can have her. We will not stop you. You may even come to our house for dinner if you like. We have a marvelous cook. You may see our Mimi any time you desire. No, Mr. Fliegelman. We would not stand in the way of anyone's desire. We are not that kind of man. Desire all you want, Mr. Fliegelman. We will not stop you."

Nion paused, sucked the end of his pen.

"We will sue you, Fliegelman," he said. "We will sue you for everything you are worth."

Fliegelman waited, knowing that Nion's threat still had some power left.

"And we can sue you, you know," he said. "That is our specialty. And when we are done suing you, you will never want anything again, seeing how painlessly it can be taken from you. You see, Fliegelman. We own it all anyway, and we will take it from you any time we choose."

Fliegelman at last spoke up.

"Nion, my good friend, my Mr. LeClair, my buddy, my pal," he said, trying to keep his laughter from mixing it up with threat's hoods. "Sue me for all you are worth. There is nothing to take. I am broke."

"You are wrong again, Mr. Fliegelman," Nion said, threat sitting heavy on the mister part of his breath. "You are a very rich man. May we show you?"

Nion reached into his flawless suit and pulled out a crisp piece of paper as big as a dollar bill and handed it to Fliegelman. It was a check, made out to Fliegelman. He gawked at the numbers.

"That's right, my friend," he said, his threat chuckling. "It's the magic number. The big six zeroes, the one we are all looking for. It is our dream. It is the one thing that we all spend our lives on. You are a millionaire, my compatriot. You are rich. Don't hesitate. You don't have to do a thing. This is the copy of the check. You've already signed it, yes, on the back, look there, and we've already deposited it in your account. It is too late. You are rich."

Fliegelman checked it out. He had signed the check; it had been deposited to his account. He was rich, and confused.

"Ah, I know," said Nion, "you're probably wondering why. Well, Fliegelman, we are not stupid. We know you. We know you are a dangerous man. You are a threat to us. We know you used to be in business, and we know who you worked for. We know they are our biggest competition, and we know you have spied on us, Fliegelman. You have seen our biggest, most important project, have you not? You have seen what we can do. You have seen what is so new and so powerful we have not even named it yet. Our Mimi showed it to you, and it was how we caught you. We are bribing you, Fliegelman, and you have already accepted us. You will tell no one now because we own you. You are rich for your indiscretions. You are one of us."

Nion glowed, gloating; Fliegelman frowned.

"Now are we through?" he asked Fliegelman. "No, we

are not. Because we can now sue you, Fliegelman. We can sue you for every penny we've given you. Do you understand?''

He did not.

''Let us explain,'' Nion said, swiveling. ''We will sue you for endangerment of our emotional attachments, Mr. Fliegelman. We will sue you for stealing Mimi away from us. Emotions are very important to us, you see, and you have stolen ours. We will sue to get them back. What is life without these emotions? It is where we make our biggest killing. It is our life blood, and we cannot afford to have someone like you stealing our emotions. We can afford to have no one steal our emotions—book clerk or bank president. We have to protect ourselves, Mr. Fliegelman. You have upset things, you see, and we must right them.''

''I will not be litigant, Mr. LeClair,'' said Fliegelman, walking away.

''You will, too, you little Fliegelman person, you,'' Nion said, standing now and shaking his pointed argument at Fliegelman. ''You will be litigized by us because we have it in our power to do so, to make you culpable and to make you financially responsible. We've already done that, and we will do more, we promise you that. We will sue Mimi, you see, and she will have no choice but to forgo you, Fliegelman. We will sue her for the return on her emotions that is our due. We will sue her for all she is worth. And we will buy you again, Fliegelman, because we own you. We own your little bookstore, or we will should we decide. And we will own your little apartment, too. We will have you one way or the other. And why, Mr. Fliegelman, why?''

Fliegelman stood rigid, unfaltering.

"This is the beauty of it, you see?" said Nion, talking circles around his desk and Fliegelman's position. "Why? Because it is our legal right, and we will not let anyone stand in the way of our legal rights. We will because we can. No one will stop us, that's why. We are civilized men, Mr. Fliegelman, and who would dare to say a thing. We do not kill, we own. That is the beauty of it, Mr. Fliegelman. We are civilized men."

Fliegelman felt the threat take sudden leave. He relaxed his posture. This office meeting had ended.

"Now, Mr. Fliegelman," said Nion, brushing sightless dust from his suit's sleeves. "I have other pressing matters, and I'm afraid I've spent all the time with you that I am able to right now. Thank you for coming, and we'll see you in court, Mr. Fliegelman."

Nion shook Fliegelman's limp hand as Fliegelman turned toward the elevator to leave.

"This way, if you please, Mr. Fliegelman," Nion said, leading him to a door between panes of glass. "The stairs please. There are important people coming."

Fliegelman walked down the twenty-four or so flights of stone fire stairs. When he opened the door on the bottom landing (he'd tried the other doors, they were locked to him) he was in the parking garage, and when he made his way through the nauseous fumes and clean cars of the underground garage, he climbed a steep ramp that led him to the back alley of the towers, where day had run off with its tail between its legs, and night had hidden itself in the corners of this dank corridor.

This was the city of heartbreak. Fliegelman returned to his apartment and faked the coughing call to work for days and nights. He locked himself in. To complicate things, the days had moved too quickly through the season of changes, the season of the scents of decay washed clean, and had gone on to the next season, early, as if the days were being sued as accomplices for their part in the endangerment of affections. The days that Fliegelman and Mimi had shared were gone. The days that came in their place were the days of whipped weather, cold rains that nipped at necks and ankles, hostile wind forces, days to hide from. The days shook Fliegelman's windows and rattled his doorknobs, trying to convince him that they were his friends and that they wanted to play with him. But Fliegelman was on to lots of things these days, and he played the sick child. He stayed inside, furnished himself with heat, and waited for the phone to ring.

Nion served papers on him, as promised, but Fliegelman took care to carry them as far as the kitchen garbage. Nothing came of his refusals, in fact, everything went as smooth as clockwork paperwork. Fliegelman read about it in the daily. Each morning, as he faced the breaking day with coffee and dread, he saw reports of his trial and read his misspelled name. He was big news in small print, usually columned between recipes and stock tips. The city's paper had long given up trying to separate its alleged stories by importance or subject; they alphabetized it now.

Fliegelman was The LeClair Affair. He was the millionaire business dropout. Nion was a bastion of the community. Mimi was the deceived socialite. The lawyers spent two days examining the evidence, mostly videotapes, which were acceptable to the court. This coincided with Nion's company's announcement of their new interactive video system, the U/R Video III. The day after the news conference there was a report, separately filed, that stock in Nion's company had nearly trebled.

After the civil court had seen the evidence, they found Fliegelman exceedingly guilty. Fliegelman's lawyer, hired by Nion to represent the vacant Fliegelman, hoped to argue for a reasonable settlement. The settlement portion of the trial lasted nearly a month, with each side producing banks of lawyers searching for precedents and loopholes. It was a heated debate, and for a few weeks the papers reported that Fliegelman might get away with everything. In the end Nion won outright, being awarded all of Fliegelman's personal assets of slightly over one million dollars. He was an admired man; he had taken the witness stand to make his own last stand. Fliegelman's absence from the courtroom was mentioned only once, and he never received any calls from anyone about the proceedings. He was banished from millionaire status, held up as an example to others. He lost badly, though his lawyer claimed there would be an appeal, for, in his words, there had been a serious miscarriage of justice, and the defense had no plans to abort their case at this time. The trial ended with one last flourish, a photograph of Mimi and Nion hugging tearfully on the courthouse steps with the caption "Affection Restored."

In a separate courthouse, during the same time of Fliegelman's trial, Nion sued Mimi, as he had promised. He won the case hands down. It only lasted a few days. Mimi's lawyer agreed to Nion's lawyer's demands that Mimi make affectionate recompensation to Nion and continue her emotional support of him for an unspecified amount of time to be worked out at a later date. This agreement was reached with neither Nion nor Mimi appearing in the courtroom, for they were too busy witnessing at Fliegelman's trial. Mimi was bound to love Nion, the judgment said. If she did not, she would lose her interest in Nion's vast personal holdings.

The days went by viciously. Fliegelman warded them off as best he could. He stayed in his apartment in his bedroom in his bed in his hiding. He had not lost his desire. It had been stolen from him, and the rapid wind caused by that theft had chilled him through and through and brought him down with an unconquerable cold heart.

Of course, the bookstore could not wait forever, and it called him back. He went to work without his desire, and he found none there. The boxes that arrived in the mail were nothing but airy Styrofoam and the same old things. Nothing new came in. The store floundered, but didn't go belly up. There were rumors in the coffee bar that the store was being bought by a big company that had big plans for it. Fliegelman walked around the rumors. There was nothing doing.

So, that was all there was to that. Fliegelman rode to work on the lazy streetcar, worked his regular shifts, and rode the lazy streetcar back to his apartment where he hid out among his life, and when he could manage it, rose from his bed to look out his window for a fleeting glimpse of his granite church among the day's now sleeting flurries.

Though Fliegelman's phone was silent, he was half expecting Nion to phone him with more threats of action. When the phone finally did ring, shocking Fliegelman's quiet apartment, it was Mimi's long-lost voice.

"Talk to me, Mimi. Talk to me. Tell me something," he said, unable or unwilling, he wasn't sure, to restrain himself. "Where are you, Mimi? Are you breaking the law, Mimi? Please tell me what is happening, Mimi. The days hate me, Mimi."

Her answer was terse. She could not talk to him now; it was too dangerous. She could lose everything. He was to meet her on some seedy corner, as soon as he could get there, where they would be free to talk. She clicked.

Fliegelman gathered himself and his things and left the warm apartment for the day's impending gloom. The day slapped him in the face, pushed him back on his heels, tried to warn him, but Fliegelman would not listen. He leaned hard on the day and fought his way down the slipping street to the corner streetcar stop. He huddled himself in the stop's transparent shelter. He jumped up and down to ward off the wicked day, and looked far down the line for the red and white carrier. Across the street a runner, unprotected from the elemental day, ran in place at the streetlight, waiting for the change and never letting up the strenuous exercise. Except for this drenched fool and Fliegelman, the streets were wisely empty.

After several minutes Fliegelman caught the blue spark of the streetcar long blocks away. He watched the puny streetcar stop and start at the empty stations along its route, giving all the passengers who weren't there plenty of time. The streetcar grew in size as it approached Fliegelman, but as it grew it slowed, it seemed to him, to a new crawl. He hated the optical inversion.

Fliegelman got on and dug for the three magic coins

that would take him there and back again, but came up empty. The driver eyed him and slowed the streetcar. Fliegelman pocketed himself again, but came up all air. He pulled out his wallet and waved a big bill at the conductor, but the conductor only pointed to a sign that showed the true score, NO PAPER MONEY. The streetcar stopped and dumped the cold Fliegelman out three blocks from his apartment. He turned on the wind and headed back home, keeping up the pace.

He turned the apartment upside down, but he couldn't find any coins. He had enough in bills to ride the streetcar for weeks, but not enough change to ride this one very important time. The bills that stuffed his wallet were too big to be taken in by the Laundromat's change maker, and the friendly neighborhood stores simply never gave change unless you bought something, and there was nothing so cheap that would give him the right change. He would have to buy three things at three different stores to accumulate the tiny treasure. Time was running away from him. He'd have to walk.

So once more into the breaching day he went, joined to his umbrella, concentrating on the sidewalk in front of him. But the day had other plans for the heedless Fliegelman and turned his umbrella inside out three different ways. He tried to fix it, but it wouldn't bow out to his pressure, and he tossed it in a garbage can that fell over. He continued along the shortest way, through the park. He ducked into an old railroad shelter at the entrance of the park, where sleeping rags huddled together for warmth. He stood there for a bit, looking out at the nasty day, calculating the drops that hurled themselves in front of him, pulled up his collar against all the bitter injustices the day tossed around him, and left the arched shelter from the storm.

The park had been hard hit by the day's wrecking; strewn branches and lost trash were everywhere. Among the debris no one but Fliegelman walked or ran or even drove by. He trudged. The park gave way to park and park and still more wracked park, a never-ending park, Fliegelman thought, until at last he snapped out of it and began the long ascent up the crest that kept him from the other side of the city where Mimi waited on an anonymous corner.

He passed the three-story flats that lined the long street, and watched the yellow living rooms burning and the steamy kitchens fogging up the windows. He wanted to be a part of any one of these cozy rooms, even if only as some strange relative that had just popped in and had to sleep on the floor.

Hot and cold, and feeling neither, feeling only fatigue, feeling only that he wanted to lie down in the streaming gutters and build a water house to keep himself dry and safe the way Inuits built ice shelters, he reached the crest of the hill and saw the city laid out before him, drowning in the day.

To his left his church, to his right cloudy neighborhoods, and in front of him the city, shivering and drawing close on itself for warmth, the heart of the city, its tallest buildings and oldest streets. Down there was Mimi.

Mimi had assigned a corner in the oldest part of the city. It bordered on the financial district, but gained no favors from this relation, and may have even suffered from the proximity through a law of proportions. What was left of the city's Barbary Coast days were once elegant hotels and restaurants fallen to all-night diners. It was crowded with what the financiers overlooked, the hopeless, hapless, shaken down of the city. They rented by the week, looking no further than that, and asked nothing more than the sparest change to get them through their homeless days. This was the leftover hunk of town, left over from the city's first century's fabulous feast.

Because the denizens were so shortsighted in their lives, so haphazard in their forgotten constructions, people got away with murder down here. They sold one another, and stole from one another, and really did kill one another, and sometimes died from all of this and neglect, too. Upstanding citizens of the larger community avoided this part of town as best they could, but they did not ignore it entirely. They came down here to gawk and stare and peep and indulge their wildest, dark fantasies. They bought what hung on the racks and what hung around the street corners, and threw the remaining crumbs of their expensive, destructive pleasures into plastic cups for the begging. This part of the city was as used as any other. It was tough, and those who came from outside it had to play by strict house rules.

Fliegelman trudged his way to the entrance of this inner city and searched for Mimi. The buildings that loomed over him were not as tall as those of his old business world, but they were closer together, and therefore loomed tighter and less forgiving. On this awful day the buildings crouched down and leaned their heads together. It was like being underground in some devastated city of the future. He gauged each step he took and placed them carefully, for he was on foreign turf.

He paid close attention to the street signs, the way a worried commuter sticks to his paper to avoid unwanted eye contact. One slip and a thousand eyes would be all over him. He wanted to be the invisible man.

Mimi had said Ninth and Hennipen, so he followed the numbers, but he was eight away. Starting at Seventeenth, he walked the wet blocks down to his destination and discovered a disgusting inversion. Whereas in the shopping and the financial districts, the lower numbers led to higher prices and salaries, an influx of luxury, in this part of town the lower streets became more impoverished, more ragged, more willing to sell their anything they could sell to stay alive. Curiously and similarly, however, he found that as the desperation grew with the decreasing numbers, the cost of the goods sold here increased with the numerical diminishing. The needs got greater, the properties more precious, the prices jumped.

The first blocks welled over with six o'clock bars, those that opened at the earliest hours. They were ninety cent bars, where that little sum bought so much gin and granted rental rights to the bottom of the ice. Ragged men in worn coats stood in doorways and looked out on the frigid day, while behind them other ragged men in other worn coats slumped on nicked stools and slumped over their worries, trying to ignore the pressing weather. Poorly lit pool tables tried to hold everything together, and the broken jukeboxes sang the same old songs. Curls and curls of blue smoke made up the rest of the atmosphere. The men in the doorways looked past Fliegelman defiantly.

Between the bars were the diners, where dining was no art and just barely sustaining. Greasy tables and torn, vinyl stools waited on anyone who came in with the right amount for the blue-green plate special, dished up from cloudy steam tables by immigrant hands. The food stayed around a long time because the most popular items in these establishments were the bottomless cup of coffee, the cracked ashtrays, and the minimum amount of rest. They stayed open continually, not knowing who might come in next. They were sad smiles that sucked the greasy spoons. The chrome had faded, and no one had time to clean the vents. The diners in these diners sat in groups of three and read the papers left behind by the lucky souls who could afford them. There were no rushes in places like these, no frenzied attacks of lunch or dinner, just the odd meal when the time came. The only leisure here was time.

Between the bars and the diners were the hotel lobbies, where the renters watched communal TV and kept their eyes glued there, kept it all focused and fought over the switches. Upstairs behind the cardboard curtained windows, Fliegelman had no idea of what went on, and he could only guess what kind of concealed hot-plate lives happened there.

He turned on Ninth and walked quickly, trying to avoid the day which seemed to be ganging up on him, but he walked with hope now because Mimi was only blocks away. In front of him was a huge building, keeping him from Hennipen. It was the newspaper's offices, and it took up three long blocks. Fliegelman had to trace around it under its lipless, pouring roofline, cut back over in front of it and catch up with Ninth again. He finally got to Hennipen, but Mimi was nowhere to be seen.

He ducked into a diner and shook himself. Mimi's faint

voice called out from a booth near the window. She stood up calling and moved to Fliegelman, telling him he looked terrible, asking what had happened. He took off his coat, joined her in the booth, sipped on some coffee, and told her the day's sad tale. They looked at each other for a long time without saying a thing, but Fliegelman jumped in on them.

"Mimi," he said. "What is happening?" He reached across and touched her warm to the touch cheek.

"It's all over," she said. Her green eyes shined.

"No, Mimi, no, it's not," said Fliegelman, the coffee bringing him back to a place where he could think again, and in that place he found the resolve he had been wanting to grip. "No, it's not at all," he said, shaking. "We can get out of here, Mimi, we can run away. We can go south, we can sell everything."

"No, my dear Fliegelman," she said. "There are no heroics here, this is no movie. We won't blow up anything, or kill anyone, or win each other with smiling charms and good looks. We've been had, Fliegelman. It's over."

"Mimi," he said, pausing on the sounds of her name. "I have lost everything. I will not stand for this. I must do something."

"And something you will," she said. She grabbed his hands. "Listen. Nion and I are going away. We cannot stay here. We are moving. We are bound to one another. He told me we have used up this city and we have to keep ahead. We will not see each other anymore, you and I, Fliegelman. We are disappearing fast. But you have lost nothing. You will do something, and I will help you do it, Fliegelman."

She reached into her expensive purse and pulled out a

packet with Fliegelman's name on it. But before she could go on, he stopped her. His resolve wouldn't take this sitting down.

"Why do you have to go, Mimi?" he asked. "Why does he get you? It is not quite right."

"He gets me because he had me. He gets me because we made an agreement, and the city backed him up on it. He gets me because you don't need me. Now, listen. Time wastes me."

Mimi handed him the packet. It was the key to her apartment, along with a piece of parchment folded over on itself.

"Take these, Fliegelman," she said with great emphasis. "Take these and do exactly as I say. No more, no less. In two days go to the towers. When you are there unfold this paper, press it against the four marks on the windows and rub it hard against the windows. Everything will be clear then. I have discovered something, Fliegelman, and you helped me get there. I am sharing it with you. I swear, you already know it. The guard will let you in. This perfect trick is no trick. When you do it, you will see what I mean. I won't be there. I'll already be gone. Now, I have to go. Goodbye, Fliegelman. That's all, goodbye."

She got up and started to leave, but Fliegelman reeled her in.

"No, Mimi. Let me stay with you a little longer. It will be the last time. Isn't it right?"

He put his hands up to touch her hair and her face with its smashing green eyes, but she arrested him.

"No, it is not the last time, though you'll never hold me again. And it isn't right to hold me one more time. That is why I'm leaving. Trust me, Fliegelman. It is for you and for me the very best. Understand me, Fliegelman. Stay and understand me. I'll try to understand you. I'm history. Goodbye, that is all, goodbye."

Her look, her imploring, her urgency, all bade Fliegelman stay. She put on her coat, grabbed her purse and left. Fliegelman, obliging the day's plan, got up and ran after her, but she was already gone. Nothing but the street shone.

MAP OF THE **W**ORLD

□

Two days later Fliegelman went to Mimi's apartment. The days had calmed themselves, the season giving itself a break. The city stood in relief.

Mimi was right. The guard let him in with a smile. The elevator took him straight to twenty-three. The door slid open at his request. Everything was gone. The bitchin' pink surfboard was gone, the not really crystalline set of dominoes, the furniture, the decor, the Miminess, all of it was gone. It was empty. All that remained were a big brass dish, a book of matches, and a heavy atlas near the windows.

Fliegelman knelt before the windows and unfolded the piece of paper Mimi had given him. It was opaque paper, and he unfolded it slowly to save it, looking for clues along the way. It took up a big part of the floor. Covering the paper were crisscrossed lines of black, oily crayon, lines of varying thicknesses. He stared at it for a long time, but drew no conclusions from its confusion of designs. There were obviously no words on this.

He looked at the window in front of him and saw four pieces of curling tape stuck at rectangular intervals, the size of the paper. He did as Mimi instructed, attaching the paper to the window with the tape, crayon side facing away from him. He discovered two small sentences written on the back. *You've seen it all before,* one said, and *Burn this because you don't need it,* said the other.

Fliegelman picked up the atlas and used its spine to rub the paper against the window. He heard the crackling and peeling as the crayon transferred from paper to glass. He rubbed and rubbed, and rubbed a third time for good luck. When he was finished rubbing, he pulled the paper slowly away from the window, checking his efficiency, and found he had completed the design, backwards now, on the window.

He burned the paper in the big brass dish, setting off the smoke detector once, but creating no alarm in the building personnel. He was still alone in the empty apartment.

Then he stood back from the window to look at the handiwork he and Mimi had created together. Black lines crossed and crossed one another, and crossed and crossed and crossed, and for the longest time that was all they did. Fliegelman stood baffled. He walked around the apartment, staring at the huge design on the glass, but could make no sense at all of the lines and the huge web. He crossed his eyes, and that only made two messes. He squinted and saw less. There was nothing here but random connections. He stared and stared at the glass until spots of white light appeared in the sky behind the glass and swam about deliriously.

Walking the empty apartment and staring at the carpet to regain his focus, he found a nickel that had fallen behind in all the movers' commotions. He bent and picked it up. When he straightened, he looked out and saw the city beyond the glass through fuzzy black smears. The city was sharp to his eyes, sharp in its details. He picked the fattest line on the window to regroup his deciphering, and as he did, he noticed that, from where he stood with the nickel in his hand, the fat black line matched and fell onto the wires of the city's busiest streetcar line. He stopped and put the nickel down where he found it. He looked again, shifting his focus from the near to the far, and the other lines of the streetcars, clearly visible from here, began to fall into place with the thickest black lines of the design on the glass. Things were falling into place.

The thinner lines of the design partnered the wires of the city's phones. The thinnest of the lines drew comparisons with the rooflines of the city's churches he could see from here, steeple to steeple. As he began to see the places in the city that matched the very visible drawings of Mimi's map, he began to pick out more, even thinner lines of her composition. The whole city was enmeshed in this web of lines, and the lines grew more and more, thousands and thousands of the very finest lines, barely visible, but undoubtedly there on Mimi's window. The city became one under his gaze.

He rushed to the window next to the lined one, looked out on the city and realized Mimi had been right again when she said he wouldn't need the map. The lines were there, without any need of the crayon's pull. The map was before him with no legend at all.

He saw the city in its entirety, saw all the lines it drew among itself. The day helped out by staying out of the way for once; it was clear.

The streetcar lines connected the big parts of the city,

the phones and electric connected the smaller bits, and the churches held everything in perspective. Fliegelman saw the trails of cars and trucks, the faint ghost tracks of people moving along. He saw the invisible lines of the radio waves and the wind's waves that carried messages. He saw the vast weave of the airliners that connected this city to all other cities. Nothing was left out. The business towers were connected by routes of mail and messenger and other less obvious lines to every other neighborhood in the city, and all the neighborhoods were connected to all the other parts of the city. Nothing was left out. Happy families and sodden ones were tightly knit, and the lonely and the gregarious were incapable of being free from one another, no matter how hard they tried to lose the signals. He saw the city bundle up on itself, a great ball of tangled lines, each line connecting to each line, a vast confusion of lines that crossed everything, no matter where he looked. In the tiny spaces between these lines, Fliegelman saw the desire of the city, squatting in the empty places. He saw desire everywhere he looked. It was impossible to miss it.

He stood there for hours, watching the day grow on itself. He saw the city going about its work, drawing more and more lines, pulling itself closer to itself. Fliegelman felt the lines that connected him to the city. It was his city. He stood for hours at Mimi's map and memorized it, knowing he would never forget it. He tucked the map inside his coat, held the city close to his body, stole the desire and its secret hiding places, and left the empty apartment behind. He went down the fire stairs and ran through the garage, came out into the streets.

The day was getting ready to knock off, preparing for

evening's takeover, and it had a few things still to say to him. It stirred up and walked behind him, trying to push him around, trying to get to him. But Fliegelman just pulled up his jacket collar and brushed the day aside.

*Available in a Ballantine Mass Market Edition.

BENEATH THE WATERS, a novel by Oswaldo França, Júnior
AN AVAILABLE MAN, a novel by Patric Kuh
THE HOLLOW DOLL (A Little Box of Japanese Shocks), by William Bohnaker
MAX AND THE CATS, a novel by Moacyr Scliar
FLIEGELMAN'S DESIRE, a novel by Lewis Buzbee

```
        PRINTERS INC.
06/08/90      11:35   1
BOOKS  1          3   23525
FLIEGELMANS DESIRE    $  7.95
CARDS  1  0345367383
CARDS  1

           SUBTOTAL   $   2.00
           TAX        $   3.50
           TOTAL      $  13.45
           TENDERED VISA $ 0.98
           CHANGE     $  14.43
                      $  14.43
                      $   0.00

      ******THANK YOU******
```